MW00927743

THE SHOEMAKER'S APRON

CZECHOSLOVAK FOLK and FAIRY TALES

By PARKER FILLMORE

A collection of twenty stories, drawn from original sources, and chosen for their variety of subject and range of interest. Here are fairy tales conceived with all the gorgeousness of the Slavic imagination; charming little nursery tales that might be told in nurseries the world over; folk tales illustrative of the wit of a canny people; and rollicking devil tales as surprising to the Anglo-Saxon imagination as they are entertaining.

They are not in any sense academic translations, but vivid renditions by a man who, besides being a student of folklore, was an accomplished story-teller in his own right.

Originally published in 1920.

NOTE

The stories in this volume are all of Czech, Moravian, and Slovak origin, and are to be found in many versions in the books of folk tales collected by Erben, Nemcova, Kulda, Dobsinsky, Rimavsky, Benes-Trebizsky, Miksicek. I got them first by word of mouth and afterwards hunted them out in the old books. My work has been that of retelling rather than translating since in most cases I have put myself in the place of a storyteller who knows several forms of the same story, equally authentic, and from them all fashions a version of his own. It is of course always the same story although told in one form to a group of children and in another form to a group of soldiers. The audience that I hope particularly to interest is the English-speaking child.

Some few of the stories--such as Nemcova's very beautiful Twelve Months and Erben's spirited Zlatovlaska and to a less degree Nemcova's hero tale, Vitazko--are already in such definitive form that it would be profanation to "edit" them. They-- especially the first two--have been told once and for all. But the same cannot be said of most of the other stories. Nemcova's renderings are too often diffuse and inconsequential, Kulda's dry, pedantic, and homiletic. Erben, the scholarly old archivist of Prague, seems to me the greatest literary artist of them all. His chief interest in folklore was philological, but he was a poet as well as a scholar and he carried his versions of the old stories from the realm of crude folklore to the realm of art.

A small number of the present tales have appeared

in earlier English collections coming, nearly always, by way of German or French translations. In the one case they have been squeezed dry of their Slavic exuberance and in the other somewhat dandified. So I make no apology for offering them afresh.

Variants of most of the tales are, of course, to be found in other countries. Grimm's The White Snake, for instance, is a variant of Zlatovlaska. My rule of selection has been to take stories that do not have well-known variants in other languages. I have to confess that The White Snake is very well known, but here I break my own rule on account of the greater beauty of the Slavic version.

In Grimm there are also to be found variants of A Gullible World (The Shrewd Farmer), The Devil's Little Brother-in-Law (Bearskin), Clever Manka (The Peasant's Clever Daughter), The Devil's Gifts (The Magic Gifts), The Candles of Life (The Strange Godfather and Godfather Death), The Shoemaker's Apron (Brother Jolly). In all these tales the same incidents are presented but with a difference in spirit and in background that instantly marks one variant Teutonic and its fellow Slavic. Moreover, as stories, the German versions of these particular tales are neither as interesting nor as important as the Slavic versions.

Both German and Slavic versions go back, in most cases, to some early common source. Take Clever Manka, for instance, and its German variant, The Farmer's Shrewd Daughter. Clever Manka is very popular among the Czechs and Slovaks and is considered by them especially typical of their own folk wisdom and folk humor. And they are right: it is. But it would be rash to say just how early or how late this story began to be told among the peoples of the earth. The catch at the end appears in a story in the Talmud and at that time it has all the marks of a long and honorable career. The story of the devil marrying a scold, another great favorite with the Slavs, also has its Talmudic parallel in the story of Azrael, the Angel of Death, marrying a woman. The Azrael story contains many of the incidents which are used in different combinations in some half-dozen of the folk tales in the present collection. And yet when comparative folklore has said all that it has to say about variants and versions the fact remains that every people puts its own mark upon the stories that it retells. The story that, in the Talmud, is told of Azrael is Hebrew. The same story passed on down the centuries from people to people appears finally as Gentle Dora or Katcha and the Devil or The Candles of Life and then it is essentially Slavic in background, humor, and imagination.

Besides its fairy tales and folk tales the present volume contains a cluster of charming little nursery tales and a group of rollicking devil tales. It is intended as a companion volume to my earlier collection, Czechoslovak Fairy Tales. Together these two books present in English a selection of tales that are fairly representative of the folk genius of a small but highly gifted branch of the great Slav people.

P. F.

May, 1920.

CONTENTS

THE TWELVE MONTHS

THE STORY OF MARUSHKA AND THE WICKED HOLENA

THE TWELVE MONTHS

There was once a woman who had two girls. One was her own daughter, the other a stepchild. Holena, her own daughter, she loved dearly, but she couldn't bear even the sight of Marushka, the stepchild. This was because Marushka was so much prettier than Holena. Marushka, the dear child, didn't know how pretty she was and so she never understood why, whenever she stood beside Holena, the stepmother frowned so crossly.

Mother and daughter made Marushka do all the housework alone. She had to cook and wash and sew and spin and take care of the garden and look after the cow. Holena, on the contrary, spent all her time decking herself out and sitting around like a grand lady.

Marushka never complained. She did all she was told to do and bore patiently their everlasting fault-finding. In spite of all the hard work she did she grew prettier from day to day, and in spite of her lazy life Holena grew uglier.

"This will never do," the stepmother thought to herself. "Soon the boys will come courting and once they see how pretty Marushka is, they'll pay no attention at all to my Holena. We had just better do all we can to get rid of that Marushka as soon as possible."

So they both nagged Marushka all day long. They made her work harder, they beat her, they didn't give her enough to eat, they did everything they could think of to make her ugly and nasty. But all to no avail. Marushka was so good and sweet that, in spite of all their harsh treatment, she kept on growing prettier.

One day in the middle of January Holena took the notion that nothing would do but she must have a bunch of fragrant violets to put in her bodice.

"Marushka!" she ordered sharply. "I want some violets. Go out to the forest and get me some."

"Good heavens, my dear sister!" cried poor Marushka. "What can you be thinking of? Whoever heard of violets growing under the snow in January?"

"What, you lazy little slattern!" Holena shouted. "You dare to argue with me! You go this minute and if you come back without violets I'll kill you!"

The stepmother sided with Holena and, taking Marushka roughly by the shoulder, she pushed her out of the house and slammed the door.

The poor child climbed slowly up the mountain side weeping bitterly. All around the snow lay deep with no track of man or beast in any direction. Marushka wandered on and on, weak with hunger and shaking with cold.

"Dear God in heaven," she prayed, "take me to yourself away from all this suffering."

Suddenly ahead of her she saw a glowing light. She struggled towards it and found at last that it came from a great fire that was burning on the top of the mountain. Around the fire there were twelve stones, one of them much bigger and higher than the rest. Twelve men were seated on the stones. Three of them were very old and white; three were not so old; three were middle-aged; and three were beautiful youths. They did not talk. They sat silent gazing at the fire. They were the Twelve Months.

For a moment Marushka was frightened and hesitated. Then she stepped forward and said, politely:

"Kind sirs, may I warm myself at your fire? I am shaking with cold."

Great January nodded his head and Marushka reached her stiff fingers towards the flames.

"This is no place for you, my child," Great January said. "Why are you here?"

"I'm hunting for violets," Marushka answered.

"Violets? This is no time to look for violets with snow on the ground!"

"I know that, sir, but my sister, Holena, says I must bring her violets from the forest or she'll kill me and my mother says so, too. Please, sir, won't you tell me where I can find some?"

Great January slowly stood up and walked over to the youngest Month. He handed him a long staff and said:

"Here, March, you take the high seat."

So March took the high seat and began waving the staff over the fire. The fire blazed up and instantly the snow all about began to melt. The trees burst into bud; the grass revived; the little pink buds of the daisies appeared; and, lo, it was spring!

While Marushka looked, violets began to peep out from among the leaves and soon it was as if a great blue quilt had been spread on the ground.

"Now, Marushka," March cried, "there are your violets! Pick them quickly!"

Marushka was overjoyed. She stooped down and gathered a great bunch. Then she thanked the Months politely, bade them good-day, and hurried away.

Just imagine Holena and the stepmother's surprise when they saw Marushka coming home through the snow with her hands full of violets. They opened the door and instantly the fragrance of the flowers filled the cottage.

"Where did you get them?" Holena demanded rudely.

"High up in the mountain," Marushka said. "The

ground up there is covered with them."

Holena snatched the violets and fastened them in her waist. She kept smelling them herself all afternoon and she let her mother smell them, but she never once said to Marushka:

"Dear sister, won't you take a smell?"

The next day as she was sitting idle in the chimney corner she took the notion that she must have some strawberries to eat. So she called Marushka and said:

"Here you, Marushka, go out to the forest and get me some strawberries."

"Good heavens, my dear sister," Marushka said, "where can I find strawberries this time of year? Whoever heard of strawberries growing under the snow?"

"What, you lazy little slattern!" Holena shouted. "You dare to argue with me! You go this minute and if you come back without strawberries, I'll kill you!"

Again the stepmother sided with Holena and, taking Marushka roughly by the shoulder, she pushed her out of the house and slammed the door.

Again the poor child climbed slowly up the mountain side weeping bitterly. All around the snow lay deep with no track of man or beast in any direction. Marushka wandered on and on, weak with hunger and shaking with cold. At last she saw ahead of her the glow of the same fire that she had seen the day before. With happy heart she hastened to it. The Twelve Months were seated as before with Great January on the high seat.

Marushka bowed politely and said:

"Kind sirs, may I warm myself at your fire? I am shaking with cold."

Great January nodded and Marushka reached her stiff fingers towards the flames.

"But Marushka," Great January said, "why are you here again? What are you hunting now?"

"I'm hunting for strawberries," Marushka answered.

"Strawberries? But, Marushka, my child, it is winter and strawberries do not grow in the snow."

Marushka shook her head sadly.

"I know that, sir, but my sister, Holena, says I must bring her strawberries from the forest or she will kill me and my mother says so, too. Please, sir, won't you tell me where I can find some?"

Great January slowly stood up and walked over to the Month who sat opposite him. He handed him the long staff and said:

"Here, June, you take the high seat."

So June took the high seat and began waving the staff over the fire. The flames blazed high and with the heat the snow all about melted instantly. The earth grew green; the trees decked themselves in leaves; the birds began to sing; flowers bloomed and, lo, it was summer! Presently little starry white blossoms covered the ground under the beech trees. Soon these turned to fruit, first green, then pink, then red, and, with a gasp of delight, Marushka saw that they were ripe strawberries.

"Now, Marushka," June cried, "there are your strawberries! Pick them quickly!"

Marushka picked an apronful of berries. Then she thanked the Months politely, bade them good-bye, and hurried home.

Just imagine again Holena and the stepmother's surprise as they saw Marushka coming through the snow with an apronful of strawberries!

They opened the door and instantly the fragrance of the berries filled the house.

"Where did you get them?" Holena demanded rudely.

"High up in the mountain," Marushka answered, "under the beech trees."

Holena took the strawberries and gobbled and

gobbled and gobbled. Then the stepmother ate all
she wanted. But it never occurred to either of them
to say:

"Here, Marushka, you take one."

The next day when Holena was sitting idle, as
usual, in the chimney corner, the notion took her
that she must have some red apples. So she called
Marushka and said:

"Here you, Marushka, go out to the forest and get
me some red apples."

"But, my dear sister," Marushka gasped, "where can
I find red apples in winter?"

"What, you lazy little slattern, you dare to argue
with me! You go this minute and if you come back
without red apples I'll kill you!"

For the third time the stepmother sided with Holena
and, taking Marushka roughly by the shoulder,
pushed her out of the house and slammed the door.

So again the poor child went out to the forest. All
around the snow lay deep with no track of man or
beast in any direction. This time Marushka hurried
straight to the mountain top. She found the Months
still seated about their fire with Great January still
on the high stone.

Marushka bowed politely and said:

"Kind sirs, may I warm myself at your fire? I am shaking with cold."

Great January nodded and Marushka reached her stiff fingers towards the flames.

"Why are you here again, Marushka?" Great January asked. "What are you looking for now?"

"Red apples," Marushka answered. "My sister, Holena, says I must bring her some red apples from the forest or she will kill me, and my mother says so, too. Please, sir, won't you tell me where I can find some?"

Great January slowly stood up and walked over to one of the older Months. He handed him the long staff and said:

"Here, September, you take the high seat."

So September took the high seat and began waving the staff over the fire. The fire burned and glowed. Instantly the snow disappeared. The fields about looked brown and yellow and dry. From the trees the leaves dropped one by one and a cool breeze scattered them over the stubble. There were not many flowers, only wild asters on the hillside, and meadow saffron in the valleys, and under the beeches ferns and ivy. Presently Marushka spied an apple-tree weighted down with ripe fruit.

"There, Marushka," September called, "there are your apples. Gather them quickly."

Marushka reached up and picked one apple. Then she picked another.

"That's enough, Marushka!" September shouted. "Don't pick any more!"

Marushka obeyed at once. Then she thanked the Months politely, bade them good-bye, and hurried home.

Holena and her stepmother were more surprised than ever to see Marushka coming through the snow with red apples in her hands. They let her in and grabbed the apples from her.

"Where did you get them?" Holena demanded.

"High up on the mountain," Marushka answered. "There are plenty of them growing there."

"Plenty of them! And you only brought us two!" Holena cried angrily. "Or did you pick more and eat them yourself on the way home?"

"No, no, my dear sister," Marushka said. "I haven't eaten any, truly I haven't. They wouldn't let me pick any more than two. They shouted to me not to pick any more."

"I wish the lightning had struck you dead!" Holena sneered. "I've a good mind to beat you!"

After a time the greedy Holena left off her scolding to eat one of the apples. It had so delicious a flavor that she declared she had never in all her life tasted anything so good. Her mother said the same. When they had finished both apples they began to wish for more.

"Mother," Holena said, "go get me my fur cloak. I'm going up the mountain myself. No use sending that lazy little slattern again, for she would only eat up all the apples on the way home. I'll find that tree and when I pick the apples I'd like to see anybody stop me!"

The mother begged Holena not to go out in such weather, but Holena was headstrong and would go. She threw her fur cloak over her shoulders and put a shawl on her head and off she went up the mountain side.

All around the snow lay deep with no track of man or beast in any direction. Holena wandered on and on determined to find those wonderful apples. At last she saw a light in the distance and when she reached it she found it was the great fire about which the Twelve Months were seated.

At first she was frightened but, soon growing bold, she elbowed her way through the circle of men and without so much as saying: "By your leave," she put out her hands to the fire. She hadn't even the courtesy to say: "Good-day."

Great January frowned.

"Who are you?" he asked in a deep voice. "And what do you want?"

Holena looked at him rudely.

"You old fool, what business is it of yours who I am or what I want!"

She tossed her head airily and walked off into the forest.

The frown deepened on Great January's brow. Slowly he stood up and waved the staff over his head. The fire died down. Then the sky grew dark; an icy wind blew over the mountain; and the snow began to fall so thickly that it looked as if some one in the sky were emptying a huge feather-bed.

Holena could not see a step before her. She struggled on and on. Now she ran into a tree, now she fell into a snowdrift. In spite of her warm cloak her limbs began to weaken and grow numb. The snow kept on falling, the icy wind kept on blowing.

Did Holena at last begin to feel sorry that she had been so wicked and cruel to Marushka? No, she did not. Instead, the colder she grew, the more bitterly she reviled Marushka in her heart, the more bitterly she reviled even the good God Himself.

Meanwhile at home her mother waited for her and waited. She stood at the window as long as she could, then she opened the door and tried to peer through the storm. She waited and waited, but no Holena came.

"Oh dear, oh dear, what can be keeping her?" she thought to herself. "Does she like those apples so

much that she can't leave them, or what is it? I think
I'll have to go out myself and find her."

So the stepmother put her fur cloak about her
shoulders, threw a shawl over her head, and started
out.

She called: "Holena! Holena!" but no one answered.

She struggled on and on up the mountain side. All
around the snow lay deep with no track of man or
beast in any direction.

"Holena! Holena!"

Still no answer.

The snow fell fast. The icy wind moaned on.

At home Marushka prepared the dinner and looked
after the cow. Still neither Holena nor the
stepmother returned.

"What can they be doing all this time?" Marushka
thought.

She ate her dinner alone and then sat down to work
at the distaff.

The spindle filled and daylight faded and still no
sign of Holena and her mother.

"Dear God in heaven, what can be keeping them!"
Marushka cried anxiously. She peered out the

window to see if they were coming.

The storm had spent itself. The wind had died
down. The fields gleamed white in the snow and up
in the sky the frosty stars were twinkling brightly.
But not a living creature was in sight. Marushka
knelt down and prayed for her sister and mother.

The next morning she prepared breakfast for them.

"They'll be very cold and hungry," she said to
herself.

She waited for them but they didn't come. She
cooked dinner for them but still they didn't come. In
fact they never came, for they both froze to death on
the mountain.

So our good little Marushka inherited the cottage
and the garden and the cow. After a time she
married a farmer. He made her a good husband and
they lived together very happily.

ZLATOVLASKA THE GOLDEN-HAIRED

THE STORY OF YIRIK AND THE SNAKE

There was once an old king who was so wise that he was able to understand the speech of all the animals in the world. This is how it happened. An old woman came to him one day bringing him a snake in a basket.

"If you have this snake cooked," she told him, "and eat it as you would a fish, then you will be able to understand the birds of the air, the beasts of the earth, and the fishes of the sea."

The king was delighted. He made the old wise woman a handsome present and at once ordered his cook, a youth named Yirik, to prepare the "fish" for dinner.

"But understand, Yirik," he said severely, "you're to cook this 'fish,' not eat it! You're not to taste one morsel of it! If you do, you forfeit your head!"

Yirik thought this a strange order.

"What kind of a cook am I," he said to himself, "that I'm not to sample my own cooking?"

When he opened the basket and saw the "fish," he was further mystified.

"Um," he murmured, "it looks like a snake to me."

He put it on the fire and, when it was broiled to a turn, he ate a morsel. It had a fine flavor. He was about to take a second bite when suddenly he heard a little voice that buzzed in his ear these words:

"Give us some, too! Give us some, too!"

He looked around to see who was speaking but there was no one in the kitchen. Only some flies were buzzing about.

Just then outside a hissing voice called out:

"Where shall we go? Where shall we go?"

A higher voice answered:

"To the miller's barley field! To the miller's barley field!"

Yirik looked out the window and saw a gander with a flock of geese.

"Oho!" he said to himself, shaking his head. "Now I understand! Now I know what kind of 'fish' this is! Now I know why the poor cook was not to take a bite!"

He slipped another morsel into his mouth, garnished the "fish" carefully on a platter, and carried it to the king.

After dinner the king ordered his horse and told Yirik to come with him for a ride. The king rode on ahead and Yirik followed.

As they cantered across a green meadow, Yirik's horse began to prance and neigh.

"Ho! Ho!" he said. "I feel so light that I could jump over a mountain!"

"So could I," the king's horse said, "but I have to remember the old bag of bones that is perched on my back. If I were to jump he'd tumble off and break his neck."

"And a good thing, too!" said Yirik's horse. "Why not? Then instead of such an old bag of bones you'd get a young man to ride you like Yirik."

Yirik almost burst out laughing as he listened to the horses' talk, but he suppressed his merriment lest the king should know that he had eaten some of the magic snake.

Now of course the king, too, understood what the horses were saying. He glanced apprehensively at Yirik and it seemed to him that Yirik was grinning.

"What are you laughing at, Yirik?"

"Me?" Yirik said. "I'm not laughing. I was just thinking of something funny."

"Um," said the king.

His suspicions against Yirik were aroused.

Moreover he was afraid to trust himself to his horse any longer. So he turned back to the palace at once.

There he ordered Yirik to pour him out a goblet of wine.

"And I warn you," he said, "that you forfeit your head if you pour a drop too much or too little."

Yirik carefully tilted a great tankard and began filling a goblet. As he poured a bird suddenly flew into the window pursued by another bird. The first bird had in its beak three golden hairs.

"Give them to me! Give them to me! They're mine!" screamed the second bird.

"I won't! I won't! They're mine!" the first bird answered. "I picked them up!"

"Yes, but I saw them first!" the other cried. "I saw them fall as the maiden sat and combed her golden tresses. Give me two of them and I'll let you keep the third."

"No! No! No! I won't let you have one of them!"

The second bird darted angrily at the first and after a struggle succeeded in capturing one of the golden hairs. One hair dropped to the marble floor, making as it struck a musical tinkle, and the first bird escaped still holding in its bill a single hair.

In his excitement over the struggle, Yirik

overflowed the goblet.

"Ha! Ha!" said the king. "See what you've done!
You forfeit your head! However, I'll suspend
sentence on condition that you find this golden-
haired maiden and bring her to me for a wife."

Poor Yirik didn't know who the maiden was nor
where she lived. But what could he say? If he
wanted to keep his head, he must undertake the
quest. So he saddled his horse and started off at
random.

His road led him through a forest. Here he came
upon a bush under which some shepherds had
kindled a fire. Sparks were falling on an anthill
nearby and the ants in great excitement were
running hither and thither with their eggs.

"Yirik!" they cried. "Help! Help, or we shall all be
burned to death, we and our young ones in the
eggs!"

Yirik instantly dismounted, cut down the burning
bush, and put out the fire.

"Thank you, Yirik, thank you!" the ants said. "Your
kindness to us this day will not go unrewarded. If
ever you are in trouble, think of us and we will help
you."

As Yirik rode on through the forest, he came upon
two fledgling ravens lying by the path.

"Help us, Yirik, help us!" they cawed. "Our father and mother have thrown us out of the nest in yonder tall fir tree to fend for ourselves. We are young and helpless and not yet able to fly. Give us some meat to eat or we shall perish with hunger."

The sight of the helpless fledglings touched Yirik to pity. He dismounted instantly, drew his sword, and killed his horse. Then he fed the starving birds the meat they needed.

"Thank you, Yirik, thank you!" the little ravens croaked. "You have saved our lives this day. Your kindness will not go unrewarded. If ever you are in trouble, think of us and we will help you."

Yirik left the young ravens and pushed on afoot. The path through the forest was long and wearisome. It led out finally on the seashore.

On the beach two fishermen were quarreling over a big fish with golden scales that lay gasping on the sand.

"It's mine, I tell you!" one of the men was shouting. "It was caught in my net, so of course it's mine!"

To this the other one shouted back:

"But your net would never have caught a fish if you hadn't been out in my boat and if I hadn't helped you!"

"Give me this one," the first man said, "and I'll let

you have the next one."

"No! You take the next one!" the other said. "This one's mine!"

So they kept on arguing to no purpose until Yirik went up to them and said:

"Let me decide this for you. Suppose you sell me the fish and then divide the money."

He offered them all the money the king had given him for his journey. The fishermen, delighted at the offer, at once agreed. Yirik handed them over the money and then, taking the gasping fish in his hand, he threw it back into the sea.

When the fish had caught its breath, it rose on a wave and called out to Yirik:

"Thank you, Yirik, thank you. You have saved my life this day. Your kindness will not go unrewarded. If ever you are in trouble, think of me and I will help you."

With that the golden fish flicked its tail and disappeared in the water.

"Where are you going, Yirik?" the fishermen asked.

"I'm going in quest of a golden-haired maiden whom my master, the king, wished to make his wife."

"He must mean the Princess Zlatovlaska," the fishermen said to each other.

"The Princess Zlatovlaska?" Yirik repeated. "Who is she?"

"She's the golden-haired daughter of the King of the Crystal Palace. Do you see the faint outlines of an island over yonder? That's where she lives. The king has twelve daughters but Zlatovlaska alone has golden hair. Each morning at dawn a wonderful glow spreads over land and sea. That's Zlatovlaska combing her golden hair."

The fishermen conferred apart for a moment and then said:

"Yirik, you settled our dispute for us and now in return we'll row you over to the island."

So they rowed Yirik over to the Island of the Crystal Palace and left him there with the warning that the king would probably try to palm off on him one of the dark-haired princesses.

Yirik at once presented himself at the palace, got an audience with the king, and declared his mission.

"H'm," the king said. "So your master desires the hand of my daughter, the Princess Zlatovlaska, eh? H'm, h'm. Well, I see no objection to your master as a son-in-law, but of course before I entrust the princess into your hands you must prove yourself worthy. I tell you what I'll do: I'll give you three tasks to perform. Be ready for the first one tomorrow."

Early the next day the king said to Yirik:

"My daughter, Zlatovlaska, had a precious necklace of pearls. She was walking in the meadow over yonder when the string broke and the pearls rolled away in the tall grasses. Now your first task is to gather up every last one of those pearls and hand them to me before sundown."

Yirik went to the meadow and when he saw how broad it was and how thickly covered with tall grasses his heart sank for he realized that he could never search over the whole of it in one day. However, he got down on his hands and knees and began to hunt.

Midday came and he had not yet found a single pearl.

"Oh dear," he thought to himself in despair, "if only my ants were here, they could help me!"

He had no sooner spoken than a million little voices answered:

"We are here and we're here to help you!"

And sure enough there they were, the very ants that he supposed were far away!

"What do you want us to do?" they asked.

"Find me all the pearls that are scattered in this meadow. I can't find one of them."

Instantly the ants scurried hither and thither and soon they began bringing him the pearls one by one. Yirik strung them together until the necklace seemed complete.

"Are there any more?" he asked.

He was about to tie the string together when a lame ant, whose foot had been burned in the fire, hobbled up, crying:

"Wait, Yirik, don't tie the string yet! Here's the last pearl!"

Yirik thanked the ants for their help and at sundown carried the string of pearls to the king. The king counted the pearls and, to his surprise, found that not one was missing.

"You've done this well," he said. "Tomorrow I'll give you your second task."

The next day when Yirik presented himself, the king said:

"While my daughter, Zlatovlaska, was bathing in the sea, a golden ring slipped from her finger and disappeared. Your task is to find me this ring before sundown."

Yirik went down to the seashore and as he walked

along the beach his heart grew heavy as he realized the difficulty of the task before him. The sea was clear but so deep that he couldn't even see the bottom. How then could he find the ring?

"Oh dear," he said aloud, "if only the golden fish were here! It could help me."

"I am here," a voice said, "and I'm here to help you."

And there was the golden fish on the crest of a wave, gleaming like a flash of fire!

"What do you want me to do?" it said.

"Find me a golden ring that lies somewhere on the bottom of the sea."

"Ah, a golden ring? A moment ago I met a pike," the fish said, "that had just such a golden ring. Wait for me here and I'll go find the pike."

In a few moments the golden fish returned with the pike and sure enough it was Zlatovlaska's ring that the pike was carrying.

That evening at sundown the king acknowledged that Yirik had accomplished his second task.

The next day the king said:

"I could never allow my daughter, Zlatovlaska, the Golden-Haired, to go to the kingdom of your master

unless she carried with her two flasks, one filled
with the Water of Life, the other with the Water of
Death. So today for a third task I set you this: to
bring the princess a flask of the Water of Life and a
flask of the Water of Death."

Yirik had no idea which way to turn. He had heard
of the Waters of Life and Death, but all he knew
about them was that their springs were far away
beyond the Red Sea. He left the Crystal Palace and
walked off aimlessly until his feet had carried him
of themselves into a dark forest.

"If only those young ravens were here," he said
aloud, "they could help me!"

Instantly he heard a loud, "Caw! Caw!" and two
ravens flew down to him, saying:

"We are here! We are here to help you! What do
you want us to do?"

"I have to bring the king a flask of the Water of Life
and a flask of the Water of Death and I don't know
where the springs are. Do you know?"

"Yes, we know," the ravens said. "Wait here and
we'll soon fetch you water from both springs."

They flew off and in a short time returned, each
bearing a gourd of the precious water.

Yirik thanked the ravens and carefully filled his two
flasks.

As he was leaving the forest, he came upon a great spider web. An ugly spider sat in the middle of it sucking a fly. Yirik took a drop of the Water of Death and flicked it on the spider. The spider doubled up dead and fell to the ground like a ripe cherry.

Then Yirik sprinkled a drop of Living Water on the fly. The fly instantly revived, pulled itself out of the web, and flew about happy and free once again.

"Thank you, Yirik," it buzzed, "thank you for bringing me back to life. You won't be sorry. Just wait and you'll soon see that I'll reward you!"

When Yirik returned to the palace and presented the two flasks, the king said:

"But one thing yet remains. You may take Zlatovlaska, the Golden-Haired, but you must yourself pick her out from among the twelve sisters."

The king led Yirik into a great hall. The twelve princesses were seated about a table, beautiful maidens all and each looking much like the others. Yirik could not tell which was Zlatovlaska, the Golden-Haired, for each princess wore a long heavy white veil so draped over her head and shoulders that it completely covered her hair.

"Here are my twelve daughters," the king said. "One of them is Zlatovlaska, the Golden-Haired. Pick her out and you may lead her at once to your master. If you fail to pick her out, then you must depart without her."

In dismay Yirik looked from sister to sister. There was nothing to show him which was Zlatovlaska, the Golden-Haired. How was he to find out?

Suddenly he heard a buzzing in his ear and a little voice whispered:

"Courage, Yirik, courage! I'll help you!"

He turned his head quickly and there was the fly he had rescued from the spider.

"Walk slowly by each princess," the fly said, "and I'll tell you when you come to Zlatovlaska, the Golden-Haired."

Yirik did as the fly ordered. He stopped a moment before the first princess until the fly buzzed:

"Not that one! Not that one!"

He went on to the next princess and again the fly buzzed:

"Not that one! Not that one!"

So he went on from princess to princess until at last the fly buzzed out:

"Yes, that one! That one!"

So Yirik remained standing where he was and said

to the king:

"This, I think, is Zlatovlaska, the Golden-Haired."

"You have guessed right," the king said.

At that Zlatovlaska removed the white veil from her head and her lovely hair tumbled down to her feet like a golden cascade. It shimmered and glowed like the sun in the early morning when he peeps over the mountain top. Yirik stared until the brightness dimmed his sight.

The king immediately prepared Zlatovlaska, the Golden-Haired, for her journey. He gave her the two precious flasks of water; he arranged a fitting escort; and then with his blessing he sent her forth under Yirik's care.

Yirik conducted her safely to his master.

When the old king saw the lovely princess that Yirik had found for him, his eyes blinked with satisfaction, he capered about like a spring lamb, and he ordered that immediate preparations be made for the wedding. He was most grateful to Yirik and thanked him again and again.

"My dear boy," he said, "I had expected to have you hanged for your disobedience and let the ravens pick your bones. But now, to show you how grateful I am for the beautiful bride you have found me, I'm not going to have you hanged at all. Instead, I shall have you beheaded and then given a decent burial."

The execution took place at once in order to be out of the way before the wedding.

"It's a great pity he had to die," the king said as the executioner cut off Yirik's head. "He has certainly been a faithful servant."

Zlatovlaska, the Golden-Haired, asked if she might have his severed head and body. The king who was too madly in love to refuse her anything said: "Yes."

So Zlatovlaska took the body and the head and put them together. Then she sprinkled them with the Water of Death. Instantly the wound closed and soon it healed so completely that there wasn't even a scar left.

Yirik lay there lifeless but looking merely as if he were asleep. Zlatovlaska sprinkled him with the Water of Life and immediately his dead limbs stirred. Then he opened his eyes and sat up. Life poured through his veins and he sprang to his feet younger, fresher, handsomer than before.

The old king was filled with envy.

"I, too," he cried, "wish to be made young and handsome!"

He commanded the executioner to cut off his head and he told Zlatovlaska to sprinkle him afterwards with the Water of Life.

The executioner did as he was told. Then
Zlatovlaska sprinkled the old king's head and body
with the Water of Life. Nothing happened.
Zlatovlaska kept on sprinkling the Water of Life
until there was no more left.

"Do you know," the princess said to Yirik, "I
believe I should have used the Water of Death
first."

So now she sprinkled the body and head with the
Water of Death and, sure enough, they grew
together at once. But of course there was no life in
them. And of course there was no possible way of
putting life into them because the Water of Life was
all gone. So the old king remained dead.

"This will never do," the people said. "We must
have a king. And with the wedding feast and
everything prepared we simply must have a
wedding, too. If Zlatovlaska, the Golden-Haired,
cannot marry the old king, she'll have to marry
some one else. Now who shall it be?"

Some one suggested Yirik because he was young
and handsome and because, like the old king, he
could understand the birds and the beasts.

"Yirik!" the people cried. "Let Yirik be our king!"

And Zlatovlaska, the Golden-Haired, who had long
since fallen in love with handsome Yirik, consented
to have the wedding at once in order that the feast
already prepared might not be wasted.

So Yirik and Zlatovlaska, the Golden-Haired, were married and they ruled so well and they lived so happily that to this day when people say of some one: "He's as happy as a king," they are thinking of King Yirik, and when they say of some one: "She's as beautiful as a queen," they are thinking of Zlatovlaska, the Golden-Haired.

THE SHEPHERD'S NOSEGAY

THE STORY OF A PRINCESS WHO LEARNED TO SAY "PLEASE"

THE SHEPHERD'S NOSEGAY

There was once a king who had a beautiful daughter. When it was time for her to get a husband, the king set a day and invited all the neighboring princes to come and see her.

One of these princes decided that he would like to have a look at the princess before the others. So he dressed himself in a shepherd's costume: a broad-brimmed hat, a blue smock, a green vest, tight breeches to the knees, thick woolen stockings, and sandals. Thus disguised he set out for the kingdom where the princess lived. All he took with him were four loaves of bread to eat on the way.

He hadn't gone far before he met a beggar who begged him, in God's name, for a piece of bread. The prince at once gave him one of the four loaves. A little farther on a second beggar held out his hand and begged for a piece of bread. To him the prince gave the second loaf. To a third beggar he gave the third loaf, and to a fourth beggar the last loaf.

The fourth beggar said to him:

"Prince in shepherd's guise, your charity will not go unrewarded. Here are four gifts for you, one for each of the loaves of bread that you have given away this day. Take this whip which has the power of killing any one it strikes however gentle the blow. Take this beggar's wallet. It has in it some bread and cheese, but not common bread and cheese for, no matter how much of it you eat, there will always be some left. Take this shepherd's ax. If ever you have to leave your sheep alone, plant it in the earth and the sheep, instead of straying, will graze around it. Last, here is a shepherd's pipe. When you blow upon it your sheep will dance and play. Farewell and good luck go with you."

The prince thanked the beggar for his gifts and then trudged on to the kingdom where the beautiful princess lived. He presented himself at the palace as a shepherd in quest of work and he told them his name was Yan. The king liked his appearance and so the next day he was put in charge of a flock of sheep which he drove up the mountain side to pasture.

He planted his shepherd's ax in the midst of a meadow and, leaving his sheep to graze about it, he went off into the forest hunting adventures. There he came upon a castle where a giant was busy cooking his dinner in a big saucepan.

"Good-day to you," Yan said politely.

The giant, who was a rude, unmannerly fellow, bellowed out:

"It won't take me long to finish you, you young whippersnapper!"

He raised a great iron club to strike Yan but Yan, quick as thought, flicked the giant with his whip and the huge fellow toppled over dead.

The next day he returned to the castle and found another giant in possession.

"Ho, ho!" he roared on sight of Yan. "What, you young whippersnapper, back again! You killed my brother yesterday and now I'll kill you!"

He raised his great iron club to strike Yan, but Yan skipped nimbly aside. Then he flicked the giant with his whip and the huge fellow toppled over dead.

When Yan returned to the castle the third day there were no more giants about. So he wandered from room to room to see what treasures were there.

In one room he found a big chest. He struck it smartly and immediately two burly men jumped out and, bowing low before him, said:

"What does the master of the castle desire?"

"Show me everything there is to be seen," Yan ordered.

So the two servants of the chest showed him everything--jewels and treasures and gold. Then they led him out into the gardens where the most wonderful flowers in the world were blooming. Yan plucked some of these and made them into a nosegay.

That afternoon, as he drove home his sheep, he played on his magic pipe and the sheep, pairing off two by two, began to dance and frisk about him. All the people in the village ran out to see the strange sight and laughed and clapped their hands for joy.

The princess ran to the palace window and when she saw the sheep dancing two by two she, too, laughed and clapped her hands. Then the wind whiffed her a smell of the wonderful nosegay that Yan was carrying and she said to her serving maid:

"Run down to the shepherd and tell him the princess desires his nosegay."

The serving maid delivered the message to Yan, but he shook his head and said:

"Tell your mistress that whoever wants this nosegay must come herself and say: 'Yanitchko, give me that nosegay.'"

When the princess heard this, she laughed and said:

"What an odd shepherd! I see I must go myself."

So the princess herself came out to Yan and said:

"Yanitchko, give me that nosegay."

But Yan smiled and shook his head.

"Whoever wants this nosegay must say: 'Yanitchko, please give me that nosegay.'"

The Princess was a merry girl, so she laughed and said:

"Yanitchko, please give me that nosegay."

Yan gave it to her at once and she thanked him sweetly.

The next day Yan went again to the castle garden and plucked another nosegay. Then in the afternoon he drove his sheep through the village as before, playing his pipe. The princess was standing at the palace window waiting to see him. When the wind brought her a whiff of the fresh nosegay that was even more fragrant than the first one, she ran out to Yan and said:

"Yanitchko, please give me that nosegay."

But Yan smiled and shook his head.

"Whoever wants this nosegay must say: 'My dear Yanitchko, I beg you most politely please to give me that nosegay.'"

"My dear Yanitchko," the princess repeated demurely, "I beg you most politely please to give me that nosegay."

So Yan gave her the second nosegay. The princess put it in her window and the fragrance filled the village until people from far and near came to see it.

After that every day Yan gathered a nosegay for the princess and every day the princess stood at the palace window waiting to see the handsome shepherd. And always when she asked for the nosegay, she said: "Please."

In this way a month went by and the day arrived when the neighboring princes were to come to meet the princess. They were to come in fine array, the people said, and the princess had ready a kerchief and a ring for the one who would please her most.

Yan planted the ax in the meadow and, leaving the sheep to graze about it, went to the castle where he ordered the servants of the chest to dress him as befitted his rank. They put a white suit upon him and gave him a white horse with trappings of silver.

So he rode to the palace and took his place with the other princes but behind them so that the princess had to crane her neck to see him.

One by one the various princes rode by the princess but to none of them did the princess give her kerchief and ring. Yan was the last to salute her, and instantly she handed him her favors.

Then before the king or the other suitors could speak to him, Yan put spurs to his horse and rode off.

That evening as usual when he was driving home his sheep, the princess ran out to him and said:

"Yan, it was you!"

But Yan laughed and put her off.

"How can a poor shepherd be a prince?" he asked.

The princess was not convinced and she said in another month, when the princes were to come again, she would find out.

So for another month Yan tended sheep and plucked nosegays for the merry little princess and the princess waited for him at the palace window every afternoon and when she saw him she always spoke to him politely and said: "Please."

When the day for the second meeting of the princes came, the servants of the chest arrayed Yan in a suit of red and gave him a sorrel horse with trappings of gold. Yan again rode to the palace and took his place with the other princes but behind them so that the princess had to crane her neck to see him.

Again the suitors rode by the princess one by one, but at each of them she shook her head impatiently and kept her kerchief and ring until Yan saluted her.

Instantly the ceremony was over, Yan put spurs to his horse and rode off and, although the king sent after him to bring him back, Yan was able to escape.

That evening when he was driving home his sheep the princess ran out to him and said:

"Yanitchko, it was you! I know it was!"

But again Yan laughed and put her off and asked her how she could think such a thing of a poor shepherd.

Again the princess was not convinced and she said in another month, when the princes were to come for the third and last time, she would make sure.

So for another month Yan tended his sheep and plucked nosegays for the merry little princess and the princess waited for him at the palace window every afternoon and, when she saw him, she always said politely: "Please."

For the third meeting of the princes the servants of the chest arrayed Yan in a gorgeous suit of black and gave him a black horse with golden trappings studded in diamonds. He rode to the palace and took his place behind the other suitors. Things went as before and again the princess saved her kerchief and ring for him.

This time when he tried to ride off the other suitors surrounded him and, before he escaped, one of them wounded him on the foot.

He galloped back to the castle in the forest, dressed once again in his shepherd's clothes, and returned to the meadow where his sheep were grazing. There he sat down and bound up his wounded foot in the kerchief which the princess had given him. Then, when he had eaten some bread and cheese from his magic wallet, he stretched himself out in the sun and fell asleep.

Meanwhile the princess, who was sorely vexed that her mysterious suitor had again escaped, slipped out of the palace and ran up the mountain path to see for herself whether the shepherd were really with his sheep. She found Yan asleep and, when she saw her kerchief bound about his foot, she knew that he was the prince.

She woke him up and cried:

"You are he! You know you are!"

Yan looked at her and laughed and he asked:

"How can I be a prince?"

"But I know you are!" the princess said. "Oh, Yanitchko, dear Yanitchko, I beg you please to tell me!"

So then Yan, because he always did anything the princess asked him when she said: "Please," told her his true name and his rank.

The princess, overjoyed to hear that her dear shepherd was really a prince, carried him off to her father, the king.

"This is the man I shall marry," she said, "this and none other."

So Yan and the merry little princess were married

and lived very happily. And the people of the country when they speak of the princess always say:

"That's a princess for you! Why, even if she is a princess, she always says 'Please' to her own husband!"

VITAZKO THE VICTORIOUS

THE STORY OF A HERO WHOSE MOTHER LOVED A DRAGON

VITAZKO THE VICTORIOUS

There was once a mother who had an only son. "He shall be a hero," she said, "and his name shall be Vitazko, the Victorious."

She suckled him for twice seven years and then, to try his strength, she led him out to the forest and bade him pull up a fir-tree by the roots.

When the boy was not strong enough to do this, she took him home and suckled him for another seven years. Then when she had suckled him for thrice seven years, she led him out to the forest again and ordered him to pull up a beech-tree by its roots.

The youth laid hold on the tree and with one mighty pull uprooted it.

"Now, my son, you are strong enough," the mother said. "Now you are worthy of your name Vitazko. Forget not the mother who has suckled you for thrice seven years but, now that you are grown, take care of her."

"I will, my mother," Vitazko promised. "Only tell me what you want me to do."

"First," the mother said, "go out into the world and find me a splendid dwelling where I may live in peace and plenty."

Taking in his hand the uprooted beech-tree as a club and armed only with it, Vitazko set forth. He followed the wind here and there and the other place and it led him at last to a fine castle.

This castle was inhabited by dragons. Vitazko pounded on the castle gates but the dragons refused to admit him. Thereupon the young hero battered down the gates, pursued the dragons from room to room of the castle, and slaughtered them all.

When he had thrown the last of them over the wall, he took possession of the castle. He found nine spacious chambers and a tenth one the door of which was closed.

Vitazko opened the door and in the room he found a dragon. This dragon was a prisoner. Three iron hoops were fastened about his body and these were chained to the wall.

"Oho!" Vitazko cried. "Another dragon! What are you doing here?"

"Me?" the dragon said. "I'm not doing anything but just sitting here. My brothers imprisoned me. Unchain me, Vitazko! If you do, I will reward you richly."

"I will not!" Vitazko said. "A fine scamp you must be if your own brothers had to chain you up! No!

You stay where you are!"

With that Vitazko slammed the door in the dragon's face and left him.

Then he went for his mother and brought her to the castle.

"Here, my mother," he said, "is the dwelling I have won for you."

He took her through the nine spacious chambers and showed her everything. At the tenth door he said:

"This door is not to be opened. All the castle belongs to you except this room only. See to it that this door is never opened. If it is opened, an evil fate will overtake you."

Then Vitazko took his beechen club and went out hunting.

He was hardly gone before his mother sat down before the tenth door and said to herself over and over:

"I wonder what can be in that room that Vitazko doesn't want me to open the door."

At last when she could restrain her curiosity no longer, she opened the door.

"Mercy on us!" she said when she saw the dragon.

"Who are you? And what are you doing here?"

"Me?" the dragon said. "I'm only a poor harmless dragon. They call me Sharkan. My brothers chained me here. They would have freed me long ago but Vitazko killed them. Unchain me, dear lady, and I will reward you richly."

He begged her and cajoled her until she was half minded to do as he asked.

"You are very beautiful," Sharkan said. "If only I were free I would make you my wife."

"Ah, but what would Vitazko say to that?" the woman asked.

"Vitazko?" repeated Sharkan. "Do you fear your own son? A dutiful son he is, to give you the castle and then forbid you to enter this room! If you were to marry me, we should soon get rid of this Vitazko and then live here together in peace and merriment."

The woman listened to these cajoling words until she was completely won over.

"But how, dear Sharkan, shall I unchain you?"

He told her to go to the cellar and from a certain cask to draw him a goblet of wine. Instantly he drank the wine, bang! the first iron hoop burst asunder. He drank a second goblet, and the second iron hoop fell from him. He drank a third goblet and, lo! he was free.

Then in dismay at what she had done, the woman cried:

"Ah me, what will Vitazko say when he comes home!"

"I have thought out a plan," Sharkan said. "Listen: when he comes home pretend you're sick and refuse to eat. When he begs you to eat something, tell him that nothing can tempt you but a suckling from the Earth Sow. He will at once go out and hunt the Earth Sow and when he touches one of her sucklings, the Sow will tear him to pieces."

Sharkan remained in hiding in the tenth chamber and presently Vitazko returned from the hunt with a young buck across his shoulders. He found his mother on the bed, moaning and groaning as if in great pain.

"What is it, dear mother?" he asked. "Are you sick?"

"Aye, my son, I'm sick. Leave me and I'll die alone!"

Vitazko in alarm rubbed her hands and begged her to eat of the venison he had brought home.

"Nay, my son," she said, "venison tempts me not. Nothing can tempt my waning appetite but a suckling from the Earth Sow."

"Then, my mother, you shall have a suckling from the Earth Sow!" Vitazko cried, and instantly he rushed out in quest of the Earth Sow and her litter.

With his beech-tree in his hand he ranged back and forth through the forest hunting the Earth Sow. He came at last to a tower in which an old wise woman lived. Her name was Nedyelka and because she was good as well as wise people called her St. Nedyelka.

"Where are you going, Vitazko?" she said, when she saw the young hero.

"I'm hunting for the Earth Sow," he told her. "My mother is sick and nothing will tempt her but a suckling from the Earth Sow's litter."

Nedyelka looked at the young man kindly.

"That, my son, is a difficult task you have set yourself. However, I will help you provided you do exactly as I say."

Vitazko promised and the old woman gave him a long pointed spit.

"Take this," she said. "Now go to my stable. There you will find my horse, Tatosh. Mount him and he will carry you on the wind to where the Earth Sow lies half buried in her wallow and surrounded by her litter. Reach over and prick one of the sucklings with this spit and then sit very still without moving. The suckling will squeal and instantly the Sow will spring up and in a fury race madly around the world and back in a moment of time. Sit perfectly still and

she won't see either you or Tatosh. Then she'll tell
the litter that if one of them squeals again and
disturbs her, she will tear it to pieces. With that
she'll settle back in the wallow and go to sleep.
Then do you pick up the same little suckling on
your spit and carry it off. This time it will be afraid
to squeal. The Sow will not be disturbed and
Tatosh, my horse, will bear you safely away."

Vitazko did exactly as Nedyelka ordered. He
mounted Tatosh and the magic steed carried him
swiftly on the wind to where the Earth Sow lay
sleeping in her wallow.

With his spit, Vitazko pricked one of the sucklings
until it squealed in terror. The Earth Sow jumped up
and in fury raced madly around the world and back
in a moment of time. Tatosh stood where he was
and Vitazko sat on his back without moving. The
Earth Sow saw neither of them.

"If one of you squeals again and disturbs me," the
Earth Sow said to the litter, "I'll wake up and tear
you to pieces!"

With that she settled back in the mud and fell
asleep.

Vitazko again reached over and now he picked up
the same little suckling on the end of his spit. This
time it made no sound. Instantly Tatosh, the magic
steed, rose on the wind and flew straight home to
Nedyelka.

"How did things go?" the old woman asked.

"Just as you said they would," Vitazko told her. "See, here is the suckling."

"Good, my son. Take it home to your mother."

So Vitazko returned the spit and led Tatosh back to his stall. Then he threw the suckling over his beech-tree, thanked old St. Nedyelka, bade her good-day, and with a happy heart went home.

At the castle the mother was making merry with the dragon. Suddenly in the distance they saw Vitazko coming.

"Here he comes!" the mother cried. "Oh dear, what shall I do?"

"Don't be afraid," Sharkan advised. "We'll send him off on another quest and this time he'll surely not come back. Pretend you're sick again and tell him you're so weak that even the suckling of the Earth Sow doesn't tempt your appetite. Tell him nothing will help you but the Water of Life and the Water of Death and if he really loves you he must get you some of both. Then he'll go off hunting the Water of Life and the Water of Death and that will be the end of him."

Sharkan hid himself in the tenth chamber and Vitazko, when he entered the castle, found his mother alone.

"It's no use, my son," she moaned. "I can't eat the suckling. Nothing will help me now but the Water of Life and the Water of Death. Of course you don't love me well enough to get me some of both."

"I do! I do!" poor Vitazko cried. "There's nothing I won't get for you to make you well!"

He snatched up his beech-tree again and hurried back to St. Nedyelka.

"What is it now?" the old woman asked.

"Can you tell me, dear St. Nedyelka, where I can find the Water of Life and the Water of Death? My poor mother is still sick and she says that nothing else will cure her."

"The Waters of Life and of Death are difficult to get," Nedyelka said. "However, dear boy, I will help you. Take these two pitchers and again mount the faithful Tatosh. He will carry you to the two shores under which flow the springs of the Water of Life and the Water of Death. The right shore opens for a moment on the instant of noon and under it the Water of Life bubbles up. The left shore opens for a moment at midnight and under it lies the still pool of the Water of Death. Wait at each shore until the moment it opens. Then reach in and scoop up a pitcher of water. Be swift or the shores will close upon you and kill you."

Vitazko took the two pitchers and mounted Tatosh. The horse rose on the wind and carried Vitazko far, far away beyond the Red Sea to the two shores of which old Nedyelka had told him.

At the moment of noon the right shore opened for

an instant and Vitazko scooped up a pitcher of the Water of Life. He had scarcely time to draw back before the opening closed with a crash.

He waited at the left shore until midnight. At the moment of midnight the left shore opened for an instant. Vitazko scooped up a pitcher of water from the still pool of the Water of Death and pulled swiftly back as the opening closed.

With the two pitchers safe in his hands, Vitazko mounted Tatosh and the magic steed rising on the wind carried him home to St. Nedyelka.

"And how did things go?" the old woman asked.

"Very well," Vitazko said. "See, here are the Waters."

St. Nedyelka took the two pitchers and when Vitazko wasn't looking changed them for two pitchers of ordinary water which she told him to carry at once to his mother.

At the castle the mother and Sharkan were again making merry when from afar they saw Vitazko with two pitchers in his hands. The mother fell into a great fright and wept and tore her hair, but the dragon again reassured her.

"He's come back this time," he said, "but we'll send him off again and he'll never return. Refuse the Waters and tell him you're so sick that nothing will help you now but a sight of the bird, Pelikan. Tell him if he loves you he will go after the bird,

Pelikan, and once he goes we need never fear him again."

Vitazko when he reached the castle hurried into his mother's chamber and offered her the Waters.

"Here, dear mother, is a pitcher of the Water of Life and a pitcher of the Water of Death. Now you will get well!"

But his mother pushed both pitchers away and, moaning and groaning as if she were in great pain, she said:

"Nay, you are too late with your Water of Life and your Water of Death! I am so far gone that nothing will cure me now but a sight of the bird, Pelikan. If you really loved me you would get it for me."

Vitazko, still trusting his mother, cried out:

"Of course I love you! Of course I'll get you the bird, Pelikan, if that is what will cure you!"

So once more he snatched up his beech-tree and hurried off to St. Nedyelka.

"What is it now?" the old woman asked him.

"It's my poor mother," Vitazko said. "She's too far gone for the Water of Life and the Water of Death. Nothing will help her now but a sight of the bird, Pelikan. Tell me, kind Nedyelka, how can I get the bird, Pelikan?"

"The bird, Pelikan, my son? Ah, that is a task to capture Pelikan! However, I will help you. Pelikan is a giant bird with a long, long neck. When he shakes his wings he raises such a wind that he blows down the forest trees. Here is a gun. Take it and mount my faithful Tatosh. He will carry you far away to the vast wilderness where Pelikan lives. When you get there, note carefully from what direction the wind blows. Shoot in that direction. Then quickly push the ramrod into the barrel of the gun and leave it there and come back to me as fast as you can."

Vitazko took the gun and mounted Tatosh. The magic steed rose on the wind and carried him far off to the distant wilderness which was the home of the bird, Pelikan. There Tatosh sank to earth and Vitazko dismounted. Immediately he felt a strong wind against his right cheek. He took aim in that direction and pulled the trigger. The hammer fell and instantly Vitazko pushed the ramrod into the gun barrel. He threw the gun over his shoulder and mounted Tatosh. Tatosh rose on the wind and in a twinkling had carried him back to St. Nedyelka.

"Well, son, how did things go?" the old woman asked as usual.

"I don't know," Vitazko said. "I did as you told me. Here is the gun."

"Let me see," Nedyelka said, squinting into the gun barrel. "Ah, son, things went very well indeed! Here is Pelikan inside the barrel."

She drew something out of the gun barrel and sure enough it was the bird, Pelikan.

She gave Vitazko another gun and told him to go out and shoot an eagle. Then she told him to carry Pelikan home to his mother, but instead of giving him Pelikan she gave him the eagle.

When Sharkan and his mother saw Vitazko coming, they decided that this time they would send him after the Golden Apples. These grew in the garden of the most powerful dragon in the world.

"If Vitazko goes near him," Sharkan said, "the dragon will tear him to pieces for he knows that it was Vitazko who killed all his brother dragons."

So the mother again feigned sickness and, when Vitazko rushed in to her and offered her what he supposed was Pelikan, she moaned and groaned and pushed the bird aside.

"Too late! Too late! I'm dying!"

"Don't say that!" poor Vitazko begged. "Will nothing save you?"

"Yes, the Golden Apples that grow in the garden of Mightiest Dragon could still save me. If you really loved me you'd get them for me."

"I do love you, mother," Vitazko cried, "and I'll get you the Golden Apples wherever they are!"

So without a moment's rest he hurried back to St. Nedyelka.

"Well, son, what is it now?" the old woman asked.

Vitazko wept.

"It's my poor mother. She's still sick. Pelikan hasn't cured her. She says now that only the Golden Apples from the garden of Mightiest Dragon can cure her. Dear, kind Nedyelka, tell me, what shall I do?"

"The Golden Apples from the garden of Mightiest Dragon! Ah, my son, that will be a task for you! For this you will need every ounce of your strength and more! But never fear! I will again befriend you. Here is a ring. Put it on a finger of your right hand and when you are sore pressed twist the ring around your finger and think of me. Instantly you will have the strength of a hundred fighting men. Now take this sword, mount the faithful Tatosh, and good luck go with you."

Vitazko thanked the dear old woman, mounted Tatosh, and was soon carried far away to the garden of the dragon. A high wall surrounded the garden, so high that Vitazko could never have scaled it alone. But it is as easy for a horse like Tatosh to take a high wall as it is for a bird.

Inside the garden Vitazko dismounted and began to look for the tree that bore the Golden Apples. Presently he met a beautiful young girl who asked him what he was doing in the dragon's garden.

"I'm looking for the Golden Apples," he told her. "I want some of them for my sick mother. Do you know where they are?"

"I do indeed know where they are," the girl said, "for it is my duty to guard them. If I were to give you one the wicked dragon would tear me to pieces. I am a royal princess but I am in the dragon's power and must do as he says. Dear youth, take my advice and escape while you can. If the dragon sees you he will kill you as he would a fly."

But Vitazko was not to be dissuaded from his quest.

"Nay, sweet princess, I must get the apples."

"Well, then," she said, "I will help you all I can. Here is a precious ring. Put it on a finger of your left hand. When you are sore pressed, think of me and twist the ring and you will have the strength of a hundred men. To conquer this horrible monster you will need the strength of more than a hundred."

Vitazko put on the ring, thanked the princess, and marched boldly on. In the center of the garden he found the tree that bore the Golden Apples. Under it lay the dragon himself.

On sight of Vitazko he raised his head and bellowed out:

"Ho, you murderer of dragons, what do you want here?"

Nothing daunted, Vitazko replied:

"I am come to shake down some of the Golden Apples."

"Indeed!" the dragon roared. "Then you will have to shake them down over my dead body!"

"I shall be glad to do that!" Vitazko said, springing at the dragon and at the same time twisting around the ring on his right hand and thinking of kind old St. Nedyelka.

The dragon grappled with him and for a moment almost took him off his feet. Then Vitazko plunged the dragon into the earth up to his ankles.

Just then there was the rustling of wings overhead and a black raven cawed out:

"Which of you wants my help, you, oh Mightiest Dragon, or you, Vitazko, the Victorious?"

"Help me!" the dragon roared.

"Then what will you give me?"

"As much gold as you want."

"Nay, raven," Vitazko shouted, "help me and I will give you all the dragon's horses that are grazing over yonder in the meadow."

"Very well, Vitazko," the raven croaked. "I'll help

you. What shall I do?"

"Cool me when I'm hot," Vitazko said, "when the dragon breathes on me his fiery breath."

They grappled again and the dragon plunged Vitazko into the ground up to his ankles. Twisting the ring on his right hand and thinking of St. Nedyelka, Vitazko gripped the dragon around the waist and plunged him into the earth up to his knees.

Then they paused for breath and the raven which had dipped its wings in a fountain sat on Vitazko's head and shook down drops of cool water on his heated face.

Then Vitazko twisted the ring on his left hand, thought of the beautiful princess, and closed with the dragon again. This time with a mighty effort he gripped the dragon as if he were a stake of wood and drove him into the ground up to his very shoulders. Then quickly drawing Nedyelka's sword, he cut off the dragon's head.

At once the lovely princess came running and herself plucked two of the Golden Apples and gave them to Vitazko. She thanked him prettily for rescuing her and she said to him:

"You have saved me, Vitazko, from this fierce monster and now I am yours if you want me."

"I do want you, dear princess," Vitazko said, "and, if I could, I'd go with you at once to your father to ask you in marriage. But I cannot. I must hurry home to my sick mother. If you love me, wait for me a year and a day and I'll surely return."

The princess made him this promise and they parted.

Remembering the raven, Vitazko rode over to the meadow and slaughtered the dragon's horses. Then rising on Tatosh he flew home on the wind to St. Nedyelka.

"Well, son, how did things go?" the old woman asked.

"Gloriously!" Vitazko answered, showing her the Golden Apples. "But if the princess hadn't given me a second ring I might have been vanquished."

"Take home the Golden Apples to your mother," Nedyelka said, "and this time ride Tatosh to the castle."

So Vitazko mounted Tatosh again and flew to the castle.

Sharkan and his mother were making merry together when they saw him coming.

"Here he comes again!" the mother cried. "What shall I do? What shall I do?"

But Sharkan could think of nothing further to suggest. So without a word he hurried to the tenth

chamber where he hid himself and the woman had
to meet Vitazko as best she could.

She laid herself on the bed feigning still to be sick
and when Vitazko appeared she greeted him most
affectionately.

"My dear son, back again? And safe and sound?
Thank God!"

Then when he gave her the Golden Apples she
jumped up from the bed, pretending that the mere
sight of them had cured her.

"Ah, my dear son!" she cried, petting him and
caressing him as she used to when he was a child.
"What a hero you are!"

She prepared food and feasted him royally and
Vitazko ate and was very happy that his mother was
herself again.

When he could eat no more she took a strong
woolen cord and, as if in play, she said to him:

"Lie down, my son, and let me bind you with this
cord as once I bound your father. Let me see if you
are as strong as he was and able to break the cord."

Vitazko smiled and lay down and allowed his
mother to bind him with the woolen cord. Then he
stretched his muscles and burst the cord asunder.

"Ah, you are strong!" his mother said. "But come,

let me try again with a thin silken cord."

Suspecting nothing, Vitazko allowed his mother to
bind him hand and foot with a thin silken cord.
Then when he stretched his muscles, the cord cut
into his flesh. So he lay there, helpless as an infant.

"Sharkan! Sharkan!" the mother called.

The dragon rushed in with a sword, cut off
Vitazko's head, and hacked his body into small
pieces. He picked out Vitazko's heart and hung it by
a string from a beam in the ceiling.

Then the woman gathered together the pieces of her
son's body, tied them in a bundle, and fastened the
bundle on Tatosh who was still waiting below in the
courtyard.

"You carried him when he was alive," she said.
"Take him now that he's dead--I don't care where."

Tatosh rose on the wind and flew home to St.
Nedyelka.

The old wise woman who knew already what had
happened was waiting for him. She took the pieces
of the body from the bundle and washed them in the
Water of Death. Then she arranged them piece by
piece as they should be and they grew together until
the wounds disappeared and there were not even
any scars left. After that she sprinkled the body with
the Water of Life and, lo, life returned to Vitazko
and he stood up, well and healthy.

"Ah," he said, rubbing his eyes, "I've been asleep, haven't I?"

"Yes," Nedyelka said, "and but for me you would never have wakened. How do you feel, my son?"

"All right," Vitazko said, "except a little strange as if I had no heart."

"You have none," Nedyelka told him. "Your heart hangs by a string from a crossbeam in the castle."

She told him what had befallen him, how his mother had betrayed him and how Sharkan had cut him to pieces.

Vitazko listened but he could feel neither surprise nor grief nor anger nor anything, for how could he feel since he had no heart?

"You need your heart, my son," Nedyelka said. "You must go after it."

She disguised him as an old village piper and give him a pair of bagpipes.

"Go to the castle," she told him, "and play on these pipes. When they offer to reward you, ask for the heart that hangs by a string from the ceiling."

So Vitazko took the bagpipes and went to the castle. He played under the castle windows and his mother looked out and beckoned him in.

He went inside and played and Sharkan and his mother danced to his music. They danced and danced until they could dance no longer.

Then they gave the old piper food and drink and offered him golden money.

But Vitazko said:

"Nay, what use has an old man for gold?"

"What then can I give you?" the woman asked.

Vitazko looked slowly about the chamber as an old man would.

"Give me that heart," he said, "that hangs from the ceiling. That's all I want."

So they gave him the heart and Vitazko thanked them and departed.

He carried the heart to Nedyelka who washed it at once in the Water of Death and the Water of Life. Then she placed it in the bill of the bird, Pelikan, and Pelikan, reaching its long thin neck down Vitazko's throat, put the heart in its proper place. The heart began to beat and instantly Vitazko could again feel joy and pain and grief and happiness.

"Now can you feel?" Nedyelka asked.

"Yes," Vitazko said. "Now, thank God, I can feel again!"

"Pelikan," Nedyelka said, "for this service you shall be freed.... As for you, my son, you must go back to the castle once more and inflict a just punishment. I shall change you into a pigeon. Fly to the castle and there, when you wish to be yourself again, think of me."

So Vitazko took the form of a pigeon and flying to the castle alighted on the window-sill.

Inside the castle chamber he saw his mother fondling Sharkan.

"See!" she cried. "A pigeon is on the window-sill. Quick! Get your crossbow and shoot it!"

But before the dragon could move, Vitazko stood in the chamber.

He seized a sword and with one mighty blow cut off the dragon's head.

"And you--you wicked, faithless mother!" he cried. "What am I to do to you!"

His mother fell on her knees and begged for mercy.

"Never fear," Vitazko said. "I won't harm you. Let God judge between us."

He took his mother by the hand and led her down into the courtyard. Then he lifted the sword and said:

"Now, mother, I shall throw this sword in the air and may God judge between us which of us has been faithless to the other."

The sword flashed in the air and fell, striking straight to the heart of the guilty mother and killing her.

Vitazko buried her in the courtyard and then returned to St. Nedyelka. He thanked the old woman for all she had done for him and then, picking up his beech-tree club, he started out to find his beautiful princess.

She had long since returned to her father and many princes and heroes had come seeking her in marriage. She had put them all off, saying she would wed no one for a year and a day.

Then before the year was up Vitazko appeared and she led him at once to her father and said:

"This man will I marry, this and none other, for he it was that rescued me from the dragon."

A great wedding feast was spread and all the country rejoiced that their lovely princess was getting for a husband Vitazko, the Victorious.

FIVE NURSERY TALES

I. KURATKO THE TERRIBLE II. SMOLICHECK
III. BUDULINEK IV. THE DEAR LITTLE HEN
V. THE DISOBEDIENT ROOSTER

KURATKO THE TERRIBLE

THE STORY OF AN UNGRATEFUL CHICK

KURATKO THE TERRIBLE

There was once an old couple who had no children.

"If only we had a chick or a child of our own!"
Grandmother used to say. "Think how we could pet
it and take care of it!"

But Grandfather always answered:

"Not at all! We are very well off as we are."

At last the old black hen in the barnyard hatched out
a chick. Grandmother was delighted.

"See, Grandpa," she said, "now we have a chick of
our own!"

But Grandfather shook his head doubtfully.

"I don't like the looks of that chick. There's

something strange about it."

But Grandmother wouldn't listen. To her the chick seemed everything it should be. She called it Kuratko and petted it and pampered it as though it were an only child.

Kuratko grew apace and soon he developed an awful appetite.

"Cockadoodledoo!" he shouted at all hours of the day. "I'm hungry! Give me something to eat!"

"You mustn't feed that chick so much!" Grandfather grumbled. "He's eating us out of house and home."

But Grandmother wouldn't listen. She fed Kuratko and fed him until sure enough there came a day when there was nothing left for herself and the old man.

That was a nice how-do-you-do! Grandmother sat working at her spinning-wheel trying to forget that she was hungry, and Grandfather sat on his stool nearby too cross to speak to her.

And then, quite as though nothing were the matter, Kuratko strutted into the room, flapped his wings, and crowed:

"Cockadoodledo! I'm hungry! Give me something to eat!"

"Not another blessed thing will I ever feed you, you

greedy chick!" Grandfather shouted.

"Cockadoodledo!" Kuratko answered. "Then I'll just eat you!"

With that he made one peck at Grandfather and swallowed him down, stool and all!

"Oh, Kuratko!" Grandmother cried. "Where's Grandpa?"

"Cockadoodledo!" Kuratko remarked. "I'm still hungry. I think I'll eat you!"

And with that he made one peck at Grandmother and swallowed her down, spinning-wheel and all!

Then that terrible chick went strutting down the road, crowing merrily!

He met a washerwoman at work over her wash-tub.

"Good gracious, Kuratko!" the woman cried. "What a great big crop you've got!"

"Cockadoodledo!" Kuratko said. "I should think my crop was big for haven't I just eaten Grandmother, spinning-wheel and all, and Grandfather, stool and all? But I'm still hungry, so now I'm going to eat you!"

Before the poor woman knew what was happening, Kuratko made one peck at her and swallowed her down, wash-tub and all!

Then he strutted on down the road, crowing merrily.

Presently he came to a company of soldiers.

"Good gracious, Kuratko!" the soldiers cried. "What a great big crop you've got!"

"Cockadoodledo!" Kuratko replied. "I should think my crop was big, for haven't I just eaten a washerwoman, tub and all, Grandmother, spinning-wheel and all, and Grandfather, stool and all? But I'm still hungry, so now I'm going to eat you!"

Before the soldiers knew what was happening, Kuratko pecked at them and swallowed them down, bayonets and all, one after another, like so many grains of wheat!

Then that terrible chick went on strutting down the road, crowing merrily.

Soon he met Kotsor, the cat. Kotsor, the cat, blinked his eyes and worked his whiskers in surprise.

"Good gracious, Kuratko, what a great big crop you've got!"

"Cockadoodledo!" Kuratko said. "I should think my crop was big, for haven't I just eaten a company of soldiers, bayonets and all; a washerwoman, tub and all; Grandmother, spinning-wheel and all; and Grandfather, stool and all? But I'm still hungry, so now I'm going to eat you!"

Before Kotsor, the cat, knew what was happening, Kuratko made one peck at him and swallowed him down.

But Kotsor, the cat, was not a person to submit tamely to such an indignity. The moment he found himself inside Kuratko he unsheathed his claws and began to scratch and to tear. He worked until he had torn a great hole in Kuratko's crop. At that Kuratko, the Terrible Chick, when he tried again to crow, toppled over dead!

Then Kotsor, the cat, jumped out of Kuratko's crop; after him the company of soldiers marched out; and after them the washerwoman with her tub, Grandmother with her spinning-wheel, and Grandfather with his stool. And they all went about their business.

Kotsor, the cat, followed Grandmother and Grandfather home and begged them to give him Kuratko for his dinner.

"You may have him for all of me," Grandfather said. "But ask Grandmother. He was her little pet, not mine."

"Indeed you may have him," Grandmother said. "I see now Grandfather was right. Kuratko was certainly an ungrateful chick and I never want to hear his name again."

So Kotsor, the cat, had a wonderful dinner and to this day when he remembers it he licks his chops and combs his whiskers.

SMOLICHECK

THE STORY OF A LITTLE BOY WHO OPENED
THE DOOR

SMOLICHECK

Once upon a time there was a little boy named
Smolicheck. He lived in a little house in the woods
with a deer whose name was Golden Antlers.

Every day when Golden Antlers went out he told
Smolicheck to lock the door after him and on no
account to open it no matter who knocked.

"If you disobey me," Golden Antlers said,
"something awful may happen."

"I won't open the door," Smolicheck always
promised. "I won't open it until you come home."

Now one day there was a knock on the door.

"Oh!" Smolicheck thought to himself, "I wonder
who that is!" and he called out:

"Who's there?"

From the outside sweet voices answered:

"Smolicheck, Smolicheck, please open the door Just
a wee little crack of two fingers--no more! We'll
reach in our cold little hands to get warm, Then

leave without doing you the least bit of harm! So open, Smolicheck, please open the door!"

But Smolicheck didn't think he ought to open the door because he remembered what Golden Antlers had told him. Golden Antlers was very kind but he spanked Smolicheck when Smolicheck was disobedient. And Smolicheck didn't want to get a spanking. So he put his hands over his ears to shut out the sound of the sweet voices and that time he didn't open the door.

"You're a good boy," Golden Antlers said in the evening when he came home. "Those must have been the wicked little wood maidens. If you had opened the door they would have carried you off to their cave and then what would you have done!"

So Smolicheck was very happy to think he had obeyed Golden Antlers and he said he would never open the door to strangers, no, never!

The next day after Golden Antlers had gone out and Smolicheck was left alone, again there came a knocking on the door, and when Smolicheck called out: "Who's there?" voices sweeter than before answered:

"Smolicheck, Smolicheck, please open the door Just a wee little crack of two fingers--no more! We'll reach in our cold little hands to get warm, Then leave without doing you the least bit of harm! So open, Smolicheck, please open the door!"

Smolicheck said, no, he couldn't open the door. He

thought to himself that he would like to have one peep at the wood maidens just to see what they looked like. But he mustn't open the door even a crack, no, he mustn't!

The little wood maidens kept on begging him and shivering and shaking and telling him how cold they were, until Smolicheck felt very sorry for them.

"I don't think it would matter," he said to himself, "if I opened the door just a weeny teeny bit."

So he opened the door just a tiny crack. Instantly two little white fingers popped in, and then two more and two more and two more, and then little white hands, and then little white arms, and then, before Smolicheck knew what was happening, a whole bevy of little wood maidens were in the room! They danced around Smolicheck and they howled and they yelled and they took hold of him and dragged him out of the house and away towards the woods!

Smolicheck was dreadfully frightened and he screamed out with all his might:

"Oh, dear Golden Antlers, wherever you are In valley or mountain or pasture afar, Come quick! Don't delay! The wicked wood maidens are dragging away Your little Smolicheck! Come quick! Don't delay!"

This time by good luck the deer was not far away. When he heard Smolicheck's cry, he bounded up,

drove the little wood maidens off, and carried
Smolicheck home on his antlers.

When they got home he put Smolicheck across his
knee and gave him something--you know what!--to
make him remember not to disobey next time.
Smolicheck cried and he said he never, never, never
would open the door again no matter how sweetly
the wood maidens begged.

For some days no one came to the door. Then again
one afternoon there was a knocking and sweet
voices called out:

"Smolicheck, Smolicheck, please open the door Just
a wee little crack of two fingers--no more! We'll
reach in our cold little hands to get warm, Then
leave without doing you the least bit of harm! So
open, Smolicheck, please open the door!"

But Smolicheck pretended he didn't hear. Then
when the little wood maidens began to shake and to
shiver and to cry with the cold and to beg him to
open the door just a little crack so that they could
warm their hands, he said to them:

"No, I won't open the door, not even a teeny weeny
crack, because if I do you'll push in as you did
before and catch me and drag me off!"

The wicked little wood maidens said:

"Oh no, Smolicheck, we wouldn't do that! We'd
never think of such a thing! And besides, if we did
take you with us, you'd have a much better time

with us than you have here, shut up in a little house all alone, while Golden Antlers is off having a good time by himself. We'd give you pretty toys and we'd play with you and you'd be very happy."

Just think: Smolicheck listened to them until he believed what they said! Then he opened the door a little crack and instantly all those naughty little wood maidens pushed into the room, seized Smolicheck, and dragged him off.

They told him they would kill him if he cried for help, but nevertheless Smolicheck called out with all his might:

"Oh, dear Golden Antlers, wherever you are In valley or mountain or pasture afar, Come quick! Don't delay! The wicked wood maidens are dragging away Your little Smolicheck! Come quick! Don't delay!"

But this time Golden Antlers was far away and didn't hear him. So no one came to help Smolicheck and the wood maidens carried him off to their cave.

There, instead of playing with him, they tormented him and teased him and made faces at him. But they did give him all he wanted to eat. In fact they stuffed him with food, especially sweets. Then every day they would pinch him and say to each other:

"Sister, do you think he's fat enough yet to roast?"

Imagine poor Smolicheck's feelings when he found

they were fattening him on sweets because they expected to roast him and eat him!

Finally one day after they had been stuffing him for a long time they cut his little finger with a knife to see how fat it was.

"Yum, yum!" the wicked little wood maidens cried. "He's fat enough! Today we can roast him!"

So they took off his clothes and laid him in a kneading trough and prepared him for the oven.

Smolicheck was so frightened that he just screamed and screamed, but the louder he screamed the more the little wood maidens laughed and clapped their hands.

Just as they were pushing him into the oven, Smolicheck roared out:

"Oh, dear Golden Antlers, wherever you are In valley or mountain or pasture afar, Come quick! Don't delay! The wicked wood maidens are roasting today Your little Smolicheck! Come quick! Don't delay!"

Suddenly there was the sound of crashing branches and, before the wood maidens knew what was happening, Golden Antlers came bounding into the cave. He tossed Smolicheck upon his antlers and off he sped as swift as the wind.

When they got home, he laid Smolicheck across his

knee and gave him something--you know what!
And Smolicheck cried and said he was sorry he had
been disobedient. And he said he would never,
never, never again open the door.

And this time he never did!

BUDULINEK

THE STORY OF ANOTHER LITTLE BOY WHO OPENED THE DOOR

BUDULINEK

There was once a little boy named Budulinek. He lived with his old Granny in a cottage near a forest.

Granny went out to work every day. In the morning when she went away she always said:

"There, Budulinek, there's your dinner on the table and mind, you mustn't open the door no matter who knocks!"

One morning Granny said:

"Now, Budulinek, today I'm leaving you some soup for your dinner. Eat it when dinner time comes. And remember what I always say: don't open the door no matter who knocks."

She went away and pretty soon Lishka, the sly old mother fox, came and knocked on the door.

"Budulinek!" she called. "You know me! Open the door! Please!"

Budulinek called back:

"No, I mustn't open the door."

But Lishka, the sly old mother fox, kept on knocking.

"Listen, Budulinek," she said: "if you open the door, do you know what I'll do? I'll give you a ride on my tail!"

Now Budulinek thought to himself:

"Oh, that would be fun to ride on the tail of Lishka, the fox!"

So Budulinek forgot all about what Granny said to him every day and opened the door.

Lishka, the sly old thing, came into the room and what do you think she did? Do you think she gave Budulinek a ride on her tail? Well, she didn't. She just went over to the table and gobbled up the bowl of soup that Granny had put there for Budulinek's dinner and then she ran away.

When dinner time came Budulinek hadn't anything to eat.

In the evening when Granny came home, she said:

"Budulinek, did you open the door and let any one in?"

Budulinek was crying because he was so hungry, and he said:

"Yes, I let in Lishka, the old mother fox, and she ate

up all my dinner, too!"

Granny said:

"Now, Budulinek, you see what happens when you open the door and let some one in. Another time remember what Granny says and don't open the door."

The next morning Granny cooked some porridge for Budulinek's dinner and said:

"Now, Budulinek, here's some porridge for your dinner. Remember: while I'm gone you must not open the door no matter who knocks."

Granny was no sooner out of sight than Lishka came again and knocked on the door.

"Oh, Budulinek!" she called. "Open the door and let me in!"

But Budulinek said:

"No, I won't open the door!"

"Oh, now, Budulinek, please open the door!" Lishka begged. "You know me! Do you know what I'll do if you open the door? I'll give you a ride on my tail! Truly I will!"

Budulinek thought to himself:

"This time maybe she will give me a ride on her

tail."

So he opened the door.

Lishka came into the room, gobbled up Budulinek's porridge, and ran away without giving him any ride at all.

When dinner time came Budulinek hadn't anything to eat.

In the evening when Granny came home she said:

"Budulinek, did you open the door and let any one in?"

Budulinek was crying again because he was so hungry, and he said:

"Yes, I let in Lishka, the old mother fox, and she ate up all my porridge, too!"

"Budulinek, you're a bad boy!" Granny said. "If you open the door again, I'll have to spank you! Do you hear?"

The next morning before she went to work, Granny cooked some peas for Budulinek's dinner.

As soon as Granny was gone he began eating the peas, they were so good.

Presently Lishka, the fox, came and knocked on the door.

"Budulinek!" she called. "Open the door! I want to come in!"

But Budulinek wouldn't open the door. He took his bowl of peas and went to the window and ate them there where Lishka could see him.

"Oh, Budulinek!" Lishka begged. "You know me! Please open the door! This time I promise you I'll give you a ride on my tail! Truly I will!"

She just begged and begged until at last Budulinek opened the door. Then Lishka jumped into the room and do you know what she did? She put her nose right into the bowl of peas and gobbled them all up!

Then she said to Budulinek:

"Now get on my tail and I'll give you a ride!"

So Budulinek climbed on Lishka's tail and Lishka went running around the room faster and faster until Budulinek was dizzy and just had to hold on with all his might.

Then, before Budulinek knew what was happening, Lishka slipped out of the house and ran swiftly off into the forest, home to her hole, with Budulinek still on her tail! She hid Budulinek down in her hole with her own three children and she wouldn't let him out. He had to stay there with the three little foxes and they all teased him and bit him. And then wasn't he sorry he had disobeyed his Granny! And, oh, how he cried!

When Granny came home she found the door open and no little Budulinek anywhere. She looked high and low, but no, there was no little Budulinek. She asked every one she met had they seen her little Budulinek, but nobody had. So poor Granny just cried and cried, she was so lonely and sad.

One day an organ-grinder with a wooden leg began playing in front of Granny's cottage. The music made her think of Budulinek.

"Organ-grinder," Granny said, "here's a penny for you. But, please, don't play any more. Your music makes me cry."

"Why does it make you cry?" the organ-grinder asked.

"Because it reminds me of Budulinek," Granny said, and she told the organ-grinder all about Budulinek and how somebody had stolen him away.

The organ-grinder said:

"Poor Granny! I tell you what I'll do: as I go around and play my organ I'll keep my eyes open for Budulinek. If I find him I'll bring him back to you."

"Will you?" Granny cried. "If you bring me back my little Budulinek I'll give you a measure of rye and a measure of millet and a measure of poppy seed and a measure of everything in the house!"

So the organ-grinder went off and everywhere he

played his organ he looked for Budulinek. But he couldn't find him.

At last one day while he was walking through the forest he thought he heard a little boy crying. He looked around everywhere until he found a fox's hole.

"Oho!" he said to himself. "I believe that wicked old Lishka must have stolen Budulinek! She's probably keeping him here with her own three children! I'll soon find out."

So he put down his organ and began to play. And as he played he sang softly:

"One old fox And two, three, four, And Budulinek He makes one more!"

Old Lishka heard the music playing and she said to her oldest child:

"Here, son, give the old man a penny and tell him to go away because my head aches."

So the oldest little fox climbed out of the hole and gave the organ-grinder a penny and said:

"My mother says, please will you go away because her head aches."

As the organ-grinder reached over to take the penny, he caught the oldest little fox and stuffed him into a sack. Then he went on playing and singing:

"One old fox And two and three And Budulinek
Makes four for me!"

Presently Lishka sent out her second child with a
penny and the organ-grinder caught the second little
fox in the same way and stuffed it also into the sack.
Then he went on grinding his organ and softly
singing:

"One old fox And another for me, And Budulinek
He makes the three."

"I wonder why that old man still plays his organ,"
Lishka said and sent out her third child with a
penny.

So the organ-grinder caught the third little fox and
stuffed it also into the sack. Then he kept on playing
and singing softly:

"One old fox-- I'll soon get you!-- And Budulinek
He makes just two."

At last Lishka herself came out. So he caught her,
too, and stuffed her in with her children. Then he
sang:

"Four naughty foxes Caught alive! And Budulinek
He makes the five!"

The organ-grinder went to the hole and called
down:

"Budulinek! Budulinek! Come out!"

As there were no foxes left to hold him back, Budulinek was able to crawl out.

When he saw the organ-grinder he cried and said:

"Oh, please, Mr. Organ-Grinder, I want to go home to my Granny!"

"I'll take you home to your Granny," the organ-grinder said, "but first I must punish these naughty foxes."

The organ-grinder cut a strong switch and gave the four foxes in the sack a terrible beating until they begged him to stop and promised that they would never again do anything to Budulinek.

Then the organ-grinder let them go and he took Budulinek home to Granny.

Granny was delighted to see her little Budulinek and she gave the organ-grinder a measure of rye and a measure of millet and a measure of poppy seed and a measure of everything else in the house.

And Budulinek never again opened the door!

THE DEAR LITTLE HEN

THE STORY OF A ROOSTER THAT CHEATED

THE DEAR LITTLE HEN

Once upon a time a big Rooster and a dear little
Hen became close friends.

"Let us go to the garden," the Rooster said, "and
scratch up some seeds and worms. I tell you what
we'll do: everything you scratch up you divide with
me, and everything I scratch up I'll divide with
you."

The dear little Hen agreed to this and off they went
together to the garden.

The dear little Hen scratched and scratched and
scratched and every time she scratched up a nice fat
worm or a tasty seed she divided with the Rooster.

And the Rooster scratched and scratched and
scratched and whenever the Hen saw him scratch up
something good he divided with her. But once,
when she wasn't looking, he scratched up a big
grain of corn and without dividing it he tried to
gobble it all himself. He gobbled it so fast that it
stuck in his throat and choked him.

"Oh, dear little Hen!" he gasped. "I'm choking! Run
quick and get me some water or I'll die!"

And with that he fell over on his back and his feet
stuck straight up in the air.

The dear little Hen ran to the Well as fast as she
could and all out of breath she gasped:

"Oh Well! Give me Some Water For Rooster!
Choking! In garden! On back! Feet up! Oh dear!
He'll die!"

The Well said:

"If you want me to give you some Water, you must
go to the Dressmaker and get me a Kerchief."

So the dear little Hen ran to the Dressmaker as fast
as she could and all out of breath she gasped:

"Dressmaker! Give me Kerchief For Well For
Water For Rooster! Choking! In garden! On back!
Feet up! Oh dear! He'll die!"

The Dressmaker said:

"If you want me to give you a Kerchief, you must
go to the Shoemaker and get me a pair of Slippers."

So the dear little Hen ran to the Shoemaker as fast
as she could and all out of breath she gasped:

"Shoemaker! Give me Slippers For Dressmaker For
Kerchief For Well For Water For Rooster!
Choking! In garden! On back! Feet up! Oh dear!
He'll die!"

The Shoemaker said:

"If you want me to give you a pair of Slippers, you
must go to the Sow and get me some Bristles."

So the dear little Hen ran to the Sow as fast as she could and all out of breath she gasped:

"Oh Sow! Give me Some Bristles For Shoemaker For Slippers For Dressmaker For Kerchief For Well For Water For Rooster! Choking! In garden! On back! Feet up! Oh dear! He'll die!"

The Sow said:

"If you want me to give you some Bristles, you must go to the Brewer and get me some Malt."

So the dear little Hen ran to the Brewer as fast as she could and all out of breath she gasped:

"Oh Brewer! Give me Some Malt For Sow For Bristles For Shoemaker For Slippers For Dressmaker For Kerchief For Well For Water For Rooster! Choking! In garden! On back! Feet up! Oh dear! He'll die!"

The Brewer said:

"If you want me to give you some Malt, you must go to the Cow and get me some Cream."

So the dear little Hen ran to the Cow as fast as she could and all out of breath she gasped:

"Oh Cow! Give me Some Cream For Brewer For Malt For Sow For Bristles For Shoemaker For Slippers For Dressmaker For Kerchief For Well For Water For Rooster! Choking! In garden! On back!

Feet up! Oh dear! He'll die!"

The Cow said:

"If you want me to give you some Cream, you must go to the Meadow and get me some Grass."

So the dear little Hen ran to the Meadow as fast as she could and all out of breath she gasped:

"Oh Meadow! Give me Some Grass For Cow For Cream For Brewer For Malt For Sow For Bristles For Shoemaker For Slippers For Dressmaker For Kerchief For Well For Water For Rooster! Choking! In garden! On back! Feet up! Oh dear! He'll die!"

The Meadow said:

"If you want me to give you some Grass, you must get me some Dew from the Sky."

So the dear little Hen looked up to the Sky and said:

"Oh Sky! Dear Sky! Give me Some Dew For Meadow For Grass For Cow For Cream For Brewer For Malt For Sow For Bristles For Shoemaker For Slippers For Dressmaker For Kerchief For Well For Water For Rooster! Choking! In garden! On back! Feet up! Oh Dear! He'll die!"

The Sky pitied the dear little Hen and at once gave her some Dew.

So the Hen gave the Meadow the Dew, and the Meadow gave the Hen some Grass.

The Hen gave the Cow the Grass, and the Cow gave the Hen some Cream.

The Hen gave the Brewer the Cream, and the Brewer gave the Hen some Malt.

The Hen gave the Sow the Malt, and the Sow gave the Hen some Bristles.

The Hen gave the Shoemaker the Bristles, and the Shoemaker gave the Hen a pair of Slippers.

The Hen gave the Dressmaker the Slippers, and the Dressmaker gave the Hen a Kerchief.

The Hen gave the Well the Kerchief, and the Well gave the Hen some Water.

The Hen gave the Rooster the Water, the Water washed down the grain of corn, and thereupon the Rooster jumped up, flapped his wings, and merrily crowed:

"Cockadoodledoo!"

And after that he never again tried to cheat the dear little Hen but always whenever he scratched up a nice fat worm or a tasty seed he divided with her.

THE DISOBEDIENT ROOSTER

THE STORY OF ANOTHER LITTLE HEN

There were once a Rooster and a Hen who were very good friends. They always went about together like brother and sister.

The Rooster was headstrong and thoughtless and often did foolish things. The little Hen was very sensible and always looked after the Rooster as well as she could.

Whenever he began doing something foolish, she always said:

"Oh, my dear, you mustn't do that!"

If the Rooster had always obeyed the little Hen he would be alive to this day. But, as I have told you, he was careless and headstrong and often he refused to take the little Hen's advice.

One day in the spring he ran into the garden and just gorged and gorged on green gooseberries.

"Oh, my dear!" the little Hen cried. "You mustn't eat green gooseberries! Don't you know they'll give you a pain in your stomach!"

But the Rooster wouldn't listen. He just kept on eating gooseberry after gooseberry until at last he got a terrible pain in his stomach and then he had to stop.

"Little Hen," he cried, "help me! Oh, my stomach!
Oh! Oh!"

He was so sick that the little Hen had to give him
some hot peppermint and put a mustard plaster on
his stomach.

After that shouldn't you suppose he would do what
she told him? But he didn't. As soon as he was well
he was just as careless and disobedient as before.

One day he went out to the meadow and he just ran
and ran and ran until he got all overheated and
perspired. Then he went down to the brook and
began drinking cold water.

"Oh, my dear," the little Hen cried, "you mustn't
drink cold water while you're overheated! Wait and
cool off!"

But would the Rooster wait and cool off? No! He
just drank that cold water and drank it until he could
drink no more.

Then he got a chill and the poor little Hen had to
drag him home and put him to bed and run for the
Doctor.

The Doctor gave him bitter medicine and he didn't
get well for a long time. In fact it was winter before
he got out of the house again.

Now shouldn't you suppose that after all this the
Rooster would never again disobey the little Hen? If

only he had he would be alive to this day. Listen, now, to what happened:

One morning when he got up, he saw that ice was beginning to form on the river.

"Goody! Goody!" he cried. "Now I can go sliding on the ice!"

"Oh, my dear," the little Hen said, "you mustn't go sliding on the ice yet! It's dangerous! Wait a few days until it's frozen harder and then go sliding."

But would the Rooster listen to the little Hen? No! He just insisted on running out that very moment and sliding on the thin ice.

And do you know what happened?

The ice broke and he fell in the river and, before the little Hen could get help, he was drowned!

And it was all his own fault, too, for the little Hen had begged him to wait until the ice was safer.

THE NICKERMAN'S WIFE

THE STORY OF LIDUSHKA AND THE IMPRISONED DOVES

There was once a young housewife named
Lidushka. One day while she was washing clothes
in the river a great frog, all bloated and ugly, swam
up to her. Lidushka jumped back in fright. The frog
spread itself out on the water, just where Lidushka
had been rinsing her clothes, and sat there working
its jaws as if it wanted to say something.

"Shoo!" Lidushka cried, but the frog stayed where it
was and kept on working its jaws.

"You ugly old bloated thing! What do you want and
why do you sit there gaping at me?"

Lidushka struck at the frog with a piece of linen to
drive it off so that she could go on with her work.
The frog dived, came up at another place, and at
once swam back to Lidushka.

Lidushka tried again and again to drive it away.
Each time she struck at it, the frog dived, came up
at another place, and then swam back. At last
Lidushka lost all patience.

"Go away, you old fat thing!" she screamed. "I have
to finish my wash! Go away, I tell you, and when
your babies come I'll be their godmother! Do you
hear?"

As if it accepted this as a promise, the frog croaked:
"All right! All right! All right!" and swam off.

Some time after this, when Lidushka was again
doing her washing at the river, the same old frog
appeared not looking now so fat and bloated.

"Come! Come, my dear!" it croaked. "You
remember your promise! You said you'd be
godmother to my babies. You must come with me
now for we're having the christening today."

Lidushka, of course, had spoken jokingly, but even
so a promise is a promise and must not be broken.

"But, you foolish frog," she said, "how can I be
godmother to your babies? I can't go down in the
water."

"Yes, you can!" the old frog croaked. "Come on!
Come on! Come with me!"

It began swimming upstream and Lidushka
followed, walking along the shore and feeling every
moment more frightened.

The old frog swam on until it reached the mill-dam.
Then it said to Lidushka:

"Now, my dear, don't be afraid! Don't be afraid!
Just lift that stone in front of you. Under it you'll
find a flight of stairs that lead straight down to my
house. I'll go on ahead. Do as I say and you can't
miss the way."

The frog disappeared in the water and Lidushka lifted the stone. Sure enough there was a flight of stairs going down under the mill-dam. And what kind of stairs do you suppose they were? They were not made of wood or stone but of great solid blocks of water, laid one on another, transparent and clear as crystal.

Lidushka timidly went down one step, then another, and another, until halfway down she was met by the old frog who welcomed her with many noisy croaks.

"This way, dear godmother! This way! Don't be afraid! Don't be afraid!"

Lidushka picked up courage and took the remaining stairs more bravely. The frog then led her to its house which, like the stairs, was built of beautiful crystal water, sparkling and transparent.

Inside everything was in readiness for the christening. Lidushka at once took the baby frogs in her arms and held them during the ceremony.

After the christening came a mighty feast to which many frogs from near and far had been invited. The old frog presented them all to Lidushka and they made much ado over her, hopping about her and croaking out noisy compliments.

Fish course after fish course was served--nothing but fish, prepared in every possible manner: boiled and broiled and fried and pickled. And there was every possible kind of fish: the finest carp and pike and mullet and trout and whiting and perch and many more of which Lidushka didn't even know the names.

When she had eaten all she could, Lidushka slipped away from the other guests and wandered off alone through the house.

She opened by chance a door that led into a sort of pantry. It was lined with long shelves and on the shelves were rows and rows of little earthenware pots all turned upside down. It seemed strange to Lidushka that they should all be upside down and she wondered why.

She lifted one pot up and under it she found a lovely white dove. The dove, happy at being released, shook out its plumage, spread its wings, and flew away.

Lidushka lifted a second pot and under it there was another lovely dove which at once spread its fluttering wings and flew off as happy as its fellow.

Lidushka lifted up a third pot and there was a third dove.

"There must be doves under all these pots!" she told herself. "What cruel creature has imprisoned them, I wonder? As the dear God has given man a soul to live forever, so He has given the birds wings to fly, and He never intended them to be imprisoned under dark pots. Wait, dear doves, and I'll set you all free!"

So Lidushka lifted pot after pot and from under every one of them an imprisoned dove escaped and flew joyously away.

Just as she had lifted the last pot, the old frog came hopping in to her in great excitement.

"Oh, my dear, my dear!" she croaked. "What have you done setting free all those souls! Quick and get you a lump of dry earth or a piece of toasted bread or my husband will catch you and take your soul! Here he comes now!"

Lidushka looked up through the crystal walls of the house but could see no one coming. Then in the distance she saw some beautiful bright red streamers floating towards her on the top of the water. They came nearer and nearer.

"Oh!" she thought to herself in sudden fright. "Those must be the red streamers of a nickerman!"

Instantly she remembered the stories her grandmother used to tell her when she was a child, how the wicked nickerman lured people to their death with bright red streamers. Many an innocent maid, haying along the river, has seen the lovely streamers in the water and reached after them with her rake. That is what the nickerman wants her to do for then he can catch her and drag her down, down, down, under the water where he drowns her and takes her soul. The nickerman is so powerful that, if once he gets you, he can drown you in a teaspoon of water! But if you clutch in your hand a clod of dry earth or a piece of toasted bread, then he is powerless to harm you.

"Oh!" Lidushka cried. "Now I understand! Those white doves were the souls of poor innocents whom this wicked nickerman has drowned! God help me to escape him!"

"Hurry, my dear, hurry!" the old frog croaked. "Run up the crystal stairs and replace the stone!"

Lidushka flew up the stairs and as she reached the top she clutched a handful of dry earth. Then she replaced the stone and the water flowed over the stairs.

The nickerman spread out his red streamers close to the shore and tried to catch her, but she was not to be tempted.

"I know who you are!" she cried, holding tight her handful of dry earth. "You'll never get my soul! And you'll never again imprison under your black pots all the poor innocent souls I liberated!"

Years afterwards when Lidushka had children of her own, she used to tell them this story and say to them:

"And now, my dears, you know why it is dangerous to reach out in the water for a red streamer or a pretty water lily. The wicked nickerman may be there just waiting to catch you."

BATCHA AND THE DRAGON

THE STORY OF A SHEPHERD WHO SLEPT ALL WINTER

Once upon a time there was a shepherd who was called Batcha. During the summer he pastured his flocks high up on the mountain where he had a little hut and a sheepfold.

One day in autumn while he was lying on the ground, idly blowing his pipes, he chanced to look down the mountain slope. There he saw a most amazing sight. A great army of snakes, hundreds and hundreds in number, was slowly crawling to a rocky cliff not far from where he was lying.

When they reached the cliff, every serpent bit off a leaf from a plant that was growing there. They then touched the cliff with the leaves and the rock opened. One by one they crawled inside. When the last one had disappeared, the rock closed.

Batcha blinked his eyes in bewilderment.

"What can this mean?" he asked himself. "Where are they gone? I think I'll have to climb up there myself and see what that plant is. I wonder will the rock open for me?"

He whistled to Dunay, his dog, and left him in charge of the sheep. Then he made his way over to the cliff and examined the mysterious plant. It was something he had never seen before.

He picked a leaf and touched the cliff in the same place where the serpents had touched it. Instantly the rock opened.

Batcha stepped inside. He found himself in a huge cavern the walls of which glittered with gold and silver and precious stones. A golden table stood in the center and upon it a monster serpent, a very king of serpents, lay coiled up fast asleep. The other serpents, hundreds and hundreds of them, lay on the ground around the table. They also were fast asleep. As Batcha walked about, not one of them stirred.

Batcha sauntered here and there examining the walls and the golden table and the sleeping serpents. When he had seen everything he thought to himself:

"It's very strange and interesting and all that, but now it's time for me to get back to my sheep."

It's easy to say: "Now I'm going," but when Batcha tried to go he found he couldn't, for the rock had closed. So there he was locked in with the serpents.

He was a philosophical fellow and so, after puzzling a moment, he shrugged his shoulders and said:

"Well, if I can't get out I suppose I'll have to stay here for the night."

With that he drew his cape about him, lay down, and was soon fast asleep.

He was awakened by a rustling murmur. Thinking that he was in his own hut, he sat up and rubbed his eyes. Then he saw the glittering walls of the cavern and remembered his adventure.

The old king serpent still lay on the golden table but no longer asleep. A movement like a slow wave was rippling his great coils. All the other serpents on the ground were facing the golden table and with darting tongues were hissing:

"Is it time? Is it time?"

The old king serpent slowly lifted his head and with a deep murmurous hiss said:

"Yes, it is time."

He stretched out his long body, slipped off the golden table, and glided away to the wall of the cavern. All the smaller serpents wriggled after him.

Batcha followed them, thinking to himself:

"I'll go out the way they go."

The old king serpent touched the wall with his tongue and the rock opened. Then he glided aside and the serpents crawled out, one by one. When the last one was out, Batcha tried to follow, but the rock swung shut in his face, again locking him in.

The old king serpent hissed at him in a deep breathy voice:

"Hah, you miserable man creature, you can't get out! You're here and here you stay!"

"But I can't stay here," Batcha said. "What can I do in here? I can't sleep forever! You must let me out! I have sheep at pasture and a scolding wife at home in the valley. She'll have a thing or two to say if I'm late in getting back!"

Batcha pleaded and argued until at last the old serpent said:

"Very well, I'll let you out, but not until you have made me a triple oath that you won't tell any one how you came in."

Batcha agreed to this. Three times he swore a mighty oath not to tell any one how he had entered the cavern.

"I warn you," the old serpent said, as he opened the wall, "if you break this oath a terrible fate will overtake you!"

Without another word Batcha hurried through the opening.

Once outside he looked about him in surprise. Everything seemed changed. It was autumn when he had followed the serpents into the cavern. Now it was spring!

"What has happened?" he cried in fright. "Oh, what an unfortunate fellow I am! Have I slept through the

winter? Where are my sheep? And my wife--what
will she say?"

With trembling knees he made his way to his hut.
His wife was busy inside. He could see her through
the open door. He didn't know what to say to her at
first, so he slipped into the sheepfold and hid
himself while he tried to think out some likely story.

While he was crouching there, he saw a finely
dressed gentleman come to the door of the hut and
ask his wife where her husband was.

The woman burst into tears and explained to the
stranger that one day in the previous autumn her
husband had taken out his sheep as usual and had
never come back.

"Dunay, the dog," she said, "drove home the sheep
and from that day to this nothing has ever been
heard of my poor husband. I suppose a wolf
devoured him, or the witches caught him and tore
him to pieces and scattered him over the mountain.
And here I am left, a poor forsaken widow! Oh
dear, oh dear, oh dear!"

Her grief was so great that Batcha leaped out of the
sheepfold to comfort her.

"There, there, dear wife, don't cry! Here I am, alive
and well! No wolf ate me, no witches caught me.
I've been asleep in the sheepfold--that's all. I must
have slept all winter long!"

At sight and sound of her husband, the woman

stopped crying. Her grief changed to surprise, then to fury.

"You wretch!" she cried. "You lazy, good-for-nothing loafer! A nice kind of shepherd you are to desert your sheep and yourself to idle away the winter sleeping like a serpent! That's a fine story, isn't it, and I suppose you think me fool enough to believe it! Oh, you--you sheep's tick, where have you been and what have you been doing?"

She flew at Batcha with both hands and there's no telling what she would have done to him if the stranger hadn't interfered.

"There, there," he said, "no use getting excited! Of course he hasn't been sleeping here in the sheepfold all winter. The question is, where has he been? Here is some money for you. Take it and go along home to your cottage in the valley. Leave Batcha to me and I promise you I'll get the truth out of him."

The woman abused her husband some more and then, pocketing the money, went off.

As soon as she was gone, the stranger changed into a horrible looking creature with a third eye in the middle of his forehead.

"Good heavens!" Batcha gasped in fright. "He's the wizard of the mountain! Now what's going to happen to me!"

Batcha had often heard terrifying stories of the wizard, how he could himself take any form he wished and how he could turn a man into a ram.

"Aha!" the wizard laughed. "I see you know me! Now then, no more lies! Tell me: where have you been all winter long?"

At first Batcha remembered his triple oath to the old king serpent and he feared to break it. But when the wizard thundered out the same question a second time and a third time, and grew bigger and more horrible looking each time he spoke, Batcha forgot his oath and confessed everything.

"Now come with me," the wizard said. "Show me the cliff. Show me the magic plant."

What could Batcha do but obey? He led the wizard to the cliff and picked a leaf of the magic plant.

"Open the rock," the wizard commanded.

Batcha laid the leaf against the cliff and instantly the rock opened.

"Go inside!" the wizard ordered.

But Batcha's trembling legs refused to move.

The wizard took out a book and began mumbling an incantation. Suddenly the earth trembled, the sky thundered, and with a great hissing whistling sound a monster dragon flew out of the cavern. It was the old king serpent whose seven years were up and who was now become a flying dragon. From his huge mouth he breathed out fire and smoke. With his long tail he swished right and left among the forest trees and these snapped and broke like little twigs.

The wizard, still mumbling from his book, handed Batcha a bridle.

"Throw this around his neck!" he commanded.

Batcha took the bridle but was too terrified to act. The wizard spoke again and Batcha made one uncertain step in the dragon's direction. He lifted his arm to throw the bridle over the dragon's head, when the dragon suddenly turned on him, swooped under him, and before Batcha knew what was happening he found himself on the dragon's back and he felt himself being lifted up, up, up, above the tops of the forest trees, above the very mountains themselves.

For a moment the sky was so dark that only the fire, spurting from the dragon's eyes and mouth, lighted them on their way.

The dragon lashed this way and that in fury, he belched forth great floods of boiling water, he hissed, he roared, until Batcha, clinging to his back, was half dead with fright.

Then gradually his anger cooled. He ceased belching forth boiling water, he stopped breathing fire, his hisses grew less terrifying.

"Thank God!" Batcha gasped. "Perhaps now he'll

sink to earth and let me go."

But the dragon was not yet finished with punishing Batcha for breaking his oath. He rose still higher until the mountains of the earth looked like tiny ant-hills, still up until even these had disappeared. On, on they went, whizzing through the stars of heaven.

At last the dragon stopped flying and hung motionless in the firmament. To Batcha this was even more terrifying than moving.

"What shall I do? What shall I do?" he wept in agony. "If I jump down to earth I'll kill myself and I can't fly on up to heaven! Oh, dragon, have mercy on me! Fly back to earth and let me go and I swear before God that never again until death will I offend you!"

Batcha's pleading would have moved a stone to pity but the dragon, with an angry shake of his tail, only hardened his heart.

Suddenly Batcha heard the sweet voice of the skylark that was mounting to heaven.

"Skylark!" he called. "Dear skylark, bird that God loves, help me, for I am in great trouble! Fly up to heaven and tell God Almighty that Batcha, the shepherd, is hung in midair on a dragon's back. Tell Him that Batcha praises Him forever and begs Him to deliver him."

The skylark carried this message to heaven and God Almighty, pitying the poor shepherd, took some birch leaves and wrote on them in letters of gold. He put them in the skylark's bill and told the skylark to drop them on the dragon's head.

So the skylark returned from heaven and, hovering over Batcha, dropped the birch leaves on the dragon's head.

The dragon instantly sank to earth, so fast that Batcha lost consciousness.

When he came to himself he was sitting before his own hut. He looked about him. The dragon's cliff had disappeared. Otherwise everything was the same.

It was late afternoon and Dunay, the dog, was driving home the sheep. There was a woman coming up the mountain path.

Batcha heaved a great sigh.

"Thank God I'm back!" he said to himself. "How fine it is to hear Dunay's bark! And here comes my wife, God bless her! She'll scold me, I know, but even if she does, how glad I am to see her!"

CLEVER MANKA

THE STORY OF A GIRL WHO KNEW WHAT TO SAY

There was once a rich farmer who was as grasping and unscrupulous as he was rich. He was always driving a hard bargain and always getting the better of his poor neighbors. One of these neighbors was a humble shepherd who in return for service was to receive from the farmer a heifer. When the time of payment came the farmer refused to give the shepherd the heifer and the shepherd was forced to lay the matter before the burgomaster.

The burgomaster, who was a young man and as yet not very experienced, listened to both sides and when he had deliberated he said:

"Instead of deciding this case, I will put a riddle to you both and the man who makes the best answer shall have the heifer. Are you agreed?"

The farmer and the shepherd accepted this proposal and the burgomaster said:

"Well then, here is my riddle: What is the swiftest thing in the world? What is the sweetest thing? What is the richest? Think out your answers and bring them to me at this same hour tomorrow."

The farmer went home in a temper.

"What kind of a burgomaster is this young fellow!"

he growled. "If he had let me keep the heifer I'd have sent him a bushel of pears. But now I'm in a fair way of losing the heifer for I can't think of any answer to his foolish riddle."

"What is the matter, husband?" his wife asked.

"It's that new burgomaster. The old one would have given me the heifer without any argument, but this young man thinks to decide the case by asking us riddles."

When he told his wife what the riddle was, she cheered him greatly by telling him that she knew the answers at once.

"Why, husband," said she, "our gray mare must be the swiftest thing in the world. You know yourself nothing ever passes us on the road. As for the sweetest, did you ever taste honey any sweeter than ours? And I'm sure there's nothing richer than our chest of golden ducats that we've been laying by these forty years."

The farmer was delighted.

"You're right, wife, you're right! That heifer remains ours!"

The shepherd when he got home was downcast and sad. He had a daughter, a clever girl named Manka, who met him at the door of his cottage and asked:

"What is it, father? What did the burgomaster say?"

The shepherd sighed.

"I'm afraid I've lost the heifer. The burgomaster set us a riddle and I know I shall never guess it."

"Perhaps I can help you," Manka said. "What is it?"

So the shepherd gave her the riddle and the next day as he was setting out for the burgomaster's, Manka told him what answers to make.

When he reached the burgomaster's house, the farmer was already there rubbing his hands and beaming with self-importance.

The burgomaster again propounded the riddle and then asked the farmer his answers.

The farmer cleared his throat and with a pompous air began:

"The swiftest thing in the world? Why, my dear sir, that's my gray mare, of course, for no other horse ever passes us on the road. The sweetest? Honey from my beehives, to be sure. The richest? What can be richer than my chest of golden ducats!"

And the farmer squared his shoulders and smiled triumphantly.

"H'm," said the young burgomaster, dryly. Then he asked:

"What answers does the shepherd make?"

The shepherd bowed politely and said:

"The swiftest thing in the world is thought for
thought can run any distance in the twinkling of an
eye. The sweetest thing of all is sleep for when a
man is tired and sad what can be sweeter? The
richest thing is the earth for out of the earth come
all the riches of the world."

"Good!" the burgomaster cried. "Good! The heifer
goes to the shepherd!"

Later the burgomaster said to the shepherd:

"Tell me, now, who gave you those answers? I'm
sure they never came out of your own head."

At first the shepherd tried not to tell, but when the
burgomaster pressed him he confessed that they
came from his daughter, Manka. The burgomaster,
who thought he would like to make another test of
Manka's cleverness, sent for ten eggs. He gave them
to the shepherd and said:

"Take these eggs to Manka and tell her to have
them hatched out by tomorrow and to bring me the
chicks."

When the shepherd reached home and gave Manka
the burgomaster's message, Manka laughed and
said: "Take a handful of millet and go right back to
the burgomaster. Say to him: 'My daughter sends
you this millet. She says that if you plant it, grow it,
and have it harvested by tomorrow, she'll bring you
the ten chicks and you can feed them the ripe

grain.'"

When the burgomaster heard this, he laughed
heartily.

"That's a clever girl of yours," he told the shepherd.
"If she's as comely as she is clever, I think I'd like to
marry her. Tell her to come to see me, but she must
come neither by day nor by night, neither riding nor
walking, neither dressed nor undressed."

When Manka received this message she waited
until the next dawn when night was gone and day
not yet arrived. Then she wrapped herself in a
fishnet and, throwing one leg over a goat's back and
keeping one foot on the ground, she went to the
burgomaster's house.

Now I ask you: did she go dressed? No, she wasn't
dressed. A fishnet isn't clothing. Did she go
undressed? Of course not, for wasn't she covered
with a fishnet? Did she walk to the burgomaster's?
No, she didn't walk for she went with one leg
thrown over a goat. Then did she ride? Of course
she didn't ride for wasn't she walking on one foot?

When she reached the burgomaster's house she
called out:

"Here I am, Mr. Burgomaster, and I've come neither
by day nor by night, neither riding nor walking,
neither dressed nor undressed."

The young burgomaster was so delighted with
Manka's cleverness and so pleased with her comely

looks that he proposed to her at once and in a short time married her.

"But understand, my dear Manka," he said, "you are not to use that cleverness of yours at my expense. I won't have you interfering in any of my cases. In fact if ever you give advice to any one who comes to me for judgment, I'll turn you out of my house at once and send you home to your father."

All went well for a time. Manka busied herself in her house-keeping and was careful not to interfere in any of the burgomaster's cases.

Then one day two farmers came to the burgomaster to have a dispute settled. One of the farmers owned a mare which had foaled in the marketplace. The colt had run under the wagon of the other farmer and thereupon the owner of the wagon claimed the colt as his property.

The burgomaster, who was thinking of something else while the case was being presented, said carelessly:

"The man who found the colt under his wagon is, of course, the owner of the colt."

As the owner of the mare was leaving the burgomaster's house, he met Manka and stopped to tell her about the case. Manka was ashamed of her husband for making so foolish a decision and she said to the farmer:

"Come back this afternoon with a fishing net and

stretch it across the dusty road. When the burgomaster sees you he will come out and ask you what you are doing. Say to him that you're catching fish. When he asks you how you can expect to catch fish in a dusty road, tell him it's just as easy for you to catch fish in a dusty road as it is for a wagon to foal. Then he'll see the injustice of his decision and have the colt returned to you. But remember one thing: you mustn't let him find out that it was I who told you to do this."

That afternoon when the burgomaster chanced to look out the window he saw a man stretching a fishnet across the dusty road. He went out to him and asked:

"What are you doing?"

"Fishing."

"Fishing in a dusty road? Are you daft?"

"Well," the man said, "it's just as easy for me to catch fish in a dusty road as it is for a wagon to foal."

Then the burgomaster recognized the man as the owner of the mare and he had to confess that what he said was true.

"Of course the colt belongs to your mare and must be returned to you. But tell me," he said, "who put you up to this? You didn't think of it yourself."

The farmer tried not to tell but the burgomaster questioned him until he found out that Manka was at the bottom of it. This made him very angry. He went into the house and called his wife.

"Manka," he said, "do you forget what I told you would happen if you went interfering in any of my cases? Home you go this very day. I don't care to hear any excuses. The matter is settled. You may take with you the one thing you like best in my house for I won't have people saying that I treated you shabbily."

Manka made no outcry.

"Very well, my dear husband, I shall do as you say: I shall go home to my father's cottage and take with me the one thing I like best in your house. But don't make me go until after supper. We have been very happy together and I should like to eat one last meal with you. Let us have no more words but be kind to each other as we've always been and then part as friends."

The burgomaster agreed to this and Manka prepared a fine supper of all the dishes of which her husband was particularly fond. The burgomaster opened his choicest wine and pledged Manka's health. Then he set to, and the supper was so good that he ate and ate and ate. And the more he ate, the more he drank until at last he grew drowsy and fell sound asleep in his chair. Then without awakening him Manka had him carried out to the wagon that was waiting to take her home to her father.

The next morning when the burgomaster opened his eyes, he found himself lying in the shepherd's cottage.

"What does this mean?" he roared out.

"Nothing, dear husband, nothing!" Manka said. "You know you told me I might take with me the one thing I liked best in your house, so of course I took you! That's all."

For a moment the burgomaster rubbed his eyes in amazement. Then he laughed loud and heartily to think how Manka had outwitted him.

"Manka," he said, "you're too clever for me. Come on, my dear, let's go home."

So they climbed back into the wagon and drove home.

The burgomaster never again scolded his wife but thereafter whenever a very difficult case came up he always said:

"I think we had better consult my wife. You know she's a very clever woman."

THE BLACKSMITH'S STOOL

THE STORY OF A MAN WHO FOUND THAT DEATH WAS NECESSARY

A long time ago when Lord Jesus and the blessed St. Peter walked about together on earth, it happened one evening that they stopped at a blacksmith's cottage and asked for a night's lodging.

"You are welcome," the blacksmith said. "I am a poor man but whatever I have I will gladly share with you."

He threw down his hammer and led his guests into the kitchen. There he entertained them with a good supper and after they had eaten he said to them:

"I see that you are tired from your day's journey. There is my bed. Lie down on it and sleep until morning."

"And where will you sleep?" St. Peter asked.

"I? Don't think of me," the blacksmith said. "I'll go out to the barn and sleep on the straw."

The next morning he gave his guests a fine breakfast, and then sent them on their way with good wishes for their journey.

As they were leaving, St. Peter plucked Lord Jesus by the sleeve and whispered:

"Master, aren't you going to reward this man? He is poor but yet has treated us most hospitably."

Lord Jesus answered Peter:

"The reward of this world is an empty reward. I was thinking to prepare him a place in heaven.
However, I will grant him something now."

Then he turned to the blacksmith and said:

"Ask what you will. Make three wishes and they will be fulfilled."

The blacksmith was overjoyed. For his first wish he said:

"I should like to live for a hundred years and always be as strong and healthy as I am this moment."

Lord Jesus said:

"Very well, that will be granted you. What is your second wish?"

The blacksmith thought for a moment. Then he said:

"I wish that I may prosper in this world and always have as much as I need. May work in my shop always be as plentiful as it is today."

"This, too, will be granted you," Lord Jesus said. "Now for your third wish."

Our blacksmith thought and thought, unable at first to decide on a third wish. At last he said:

"Grant that whoever sits on the stool where you sat last night at supper may be unable to get up until I release him."

St. Peter laughed at this, but Lord Jesus nodded and said:

"This wish, too, will be fulfilled."

So they parted, Lord Jesus and blessed St. Peter going on their way, and the blacksmith returning home to his forge.

Things came to pass as Lord Jesus had promised they should. Work in plenty flowed into the blacksmith's shop. The years went by but they made no impression on the blacksmith. He was as young as ever and as vigorous. His friends grew old and one by one died. His children grew up, married, and had children of their own. These in turn grew up. The years brought youth and maturity and old age to them all. The blacksmith alone remained unchanged.

A hundred years is a long time but at last even it runs out.

One night as the blacksmith was putting away his tools, there came a knock at the door. The blacksmith stopped his singing to call out:

"Who's there?"

"It is I, Death," a voice answered. "Open the door, blacksmith. Your time has come."

The blacksmith threw open the door.

"Welcome," he said to the woman standing there. "I'll be ready in a moment when I put away my tools." He smiled a little to himself. "Won't you sit down on this stool, dear lady, and rest you for a moment? You must be weary going to and fro over the earth."

Death, suspecting nothing, seated herself on the stool.

The blacksmith burst into a loud laugh.

"Now I have you, my lady! Stay where you are until I release you!"

Death tried to stand up but could not. She squirmed this way and that. She rattled her hollow bones. She gnashed her teeth. But do what she would she could not arise from the stool.

Chuckling and singing, the blacksmith left her there and went about his business.

But soon he found that chaining up Death had unexpected results. To begin with, he wanted at once to celebrate his escape with a feast. He had a hog which had been fattening for some time. He would slaughter this hog and chop it up into fine spicy sausages which his neighbors and friends would help him eat. The hams he would hang in the chimney to smoke.

But when he tried to slaughter the animal, the blow of his axe had no effect. He struck the hog on the head and, to be sure, it rolled over on the ground. But when he stopped to cut the throat, the creature jumped up and with a grunt went scampering off. Before the blacksmith could recover from his surprise, the hog had disappeared.

Next he tried to kill a goose. He had a fat one which he had been stuffing for the village fair.

"Since those sausages have escaped me," he said. "I'll have to be satisfied with roast goose."

But when he tried to cut the goose's throat, the knife drew no blood. In his surprise he loosened his hold and the goose slipped from his hands and went cackling off after the hog.

"What's come over things today?" the blacksmith asked himself. "It seems I'm not to have sausage or roast goose. I suppose I'll have to be satisfied with a pair of pigeons."

He went out to the pigeon-house and caught two pigeons. He put them on the chopping-block and with one mighty blow of his ax cut off both their heads.

"There!" he cried in triumph. "I've got you!"

But even as he spoke the little severed heads
returned to their bodies, the heads and bodies grew
together as if nothing had happened, and cooing
happily the two pigeons flew away.

Then at last the truth flashed upon the blacksmith's
mind. So long as he kept Death fastened to that
stool, nothing could die! Of course not! So no more
spicy sausages, no more smoked hams, no more
roast goose--not even a broiled pigeon! The
prospect was not a pleasing one, for the blacksmith
loved good things to eat. But what could he do?
Release Death? Never that! He would be her first
victim! Well then, if he could have no fresh meat,
he would have to be content to live on peas and
porridge and wheaten cakes.

This actually was what he had to do and what every
one else had to do when their old provisions were
exhausted.

Summer passed and winter followed. Then spring
came bringing new and unforeseen miseries. With
the first breath of warm weather all the pests and
insects of the summer before revived, for not one of
them had been killed by the winter cold. And the
eggs they had laid all hatched out until the earth and
the air and the water swarmed with living creatures.
Birds and rats and grasshoppers, insects and bugs
and vermin of every kind, covered the fields and ate
up every green thing. The meadows looked as if a
fire had swept them clean. The orchards were
stripped bare of every leaf and blossom.

Such hordes of fish and frogs and water creatures

filled the lakes and the rivers that the water was polluted and it was impossible for man to drink it.

Water and land alike were swarming with living creatures not one of which could be killed. Even the air was thick with clouds of mosquitoes and gnats and flies.

Men and women walked about looking like tormented ghosts. They had no desire to live on but they had to live on for they could not die.

The blacksmith came at last to a realization of all the misery which his foolish wish was bringing upon the world.

"I see now," he said, "that God Almighty did well when He sent Death to the world. She has her work to do and I am wrong to hold her prisoner."

So he released Death from the stool and made no outcry when she put her bony fingers to his throat.

A GULLIBLE WORLD

THE STORY OF A MAN WHO DIDN'T BEAT HIS WIFE

There was once a poor farm laborer, so poor that all he owned in the world was a hen. He told his wife to take this hen to market and sell it.

"How much shall I ask for it?" the woman wanted to know.

"Ask as much as they'll pay, of course," the laborer said.

So the woman took the hen by the feet and set out. Near the village she met a farmer.

"Good day," the farmer said. "Where are you going with that hen?"

"I'm going to market to sell it for as much as they'll pay me."

The farmer weighed the hen in his hand, pursed his lips, thought a moment, and said:

"You better sell it to me. I'll pay you three pennies for it."

"Three pennies? Are you sure that's as much as you'll pay?"

"Yes," the farmer said, "three pennies is as much as

I'll pay."

So the laborer's wife sold the hen for three pennies.
She went on to the village and there she bought a
pretty little paper bag with one of the pennies and a
piece of ribbon with another penny. She put the
third penny into the bag, tied the bag with the
ribbon, slipped the ribbon on a stick, put the stick
over her shoulder, and then, feeling that she had
done a very good day's work, she tramped home to
her husband.

When the laborer heard how stupidly his wife had
acted, he flew into a great rage and at first
threatened to give her a sound beating.

"Was there ever such a foolish woman in the
world?" he shouted angrily.

The poor woman, who by this time was snuffling
and weeping, whimpered out:

"I don't see why you find so much fault with me!
I'm sure I'm not the only gullible person in the
world."

"Well," the laborer said, "I don't know. Perhaps
there are people in the world as gullible as you. I
tell you what I'll do: I'll go out and see if I can find
them. If I do, I won't beat you."

So the laborer went out into the world to see if he
could find any one as gullible as his wife. He
traveled several days until he reached a countryside
where he was unknown. Here he came to a fine

castle at the window of which stood the lady of the castle looking out.

"Now then, my lady," the laborer said to himself, "we'll see how gullible you are."

He stood in the middle of the road, looked intently up at the sky, and then reaching out his arms as if he were trying to catch hold of something he began jumping up and down.

The lady of the castle watched him for a few moments and then dispatched one of her servants to ask him what he was doing. The servant hurried out and questioned him and this is the story the clever rascal made up:

"I'm trying to jump back into heaven. You see I live up there. I was wrestling up there with one of my comrades and he pitched me out and now I can't find the hole I fell through."

With his eyes popping out of his head, the servant hurried back to his mistress and repeated the laborer's story word for word.

The lady of the castle instantly sent for the laborer.

"You say you were in heaven?" she asked him.

"Yes, my lady, that's where I live and I'm going back at once."

"I have a dear son in heaven," the lady said. "Do

you know him?"

"Of course I know him. The last time I saw him he was sitting far back in the chimney corner looking very sad and lonely."

"What! My son sitting far back in the chimney corner! Poor boy, he must be in need of money! My good man, will you take him something from me? I'd like to send him three hundred golden ducats and material for six fine shirts. And tell him not to be lonely as I'll come to him soon."

The laborer was delighted at the success of his yarn and he told the lady of the castle he'd gladly take with him the ducats and the fine shirting and he asked her to give them to him at once as he had to get back to heaven without delay.

The foolish woman wrapped up the shirting and counted out the money and the laborer hurried off.

Once out of sight of the castle he sat down by the roadside, stuffed the fine shirting into the legs of his trousers, and hid the ducats in his pockets. Then he stretched himself out to rest.

Meantime the lord of the castle got home and his wife at once told him the whole story and asked him if he didn't think she was fortunate to find a man who had consented to deliver to their son in heaven three hundred golden ducats and material for six fine shirts.

"What!" cried the husband. "Oh, what a gullible

creature you are! Who ever heard of a man falling out of heaven! And if he were to fall, how could he climb back? The rogue has swindled you! Which way did he go?"

And without waiting to hear the poor lady's lamentations, the nobleman mounted his horse and galloped off in the direction the laborer had taken.

The laborer, who was still resting by the wayside, saw him coming and guessed who he was.

"Now, my lord, we'll try you," he said to himself.

He took off his broad-trimmed hat and put it on the ground beside him over a clod of earth.

"My good fellow," said the nobleman, "I am looking for a man with a bundle over his shoulder. Have you seen him pass this way?"

The laborer scratched his head and pretended to think.

"Yes, master," he said, "seems to me I did see a man with a bundle. He was running over there towards the woods and looking back all the time. He was a stranger to these parts. I remember now thinking to myself that he looked like one of those rogues that come from big cities to swindle honest country folk. Yes, master, that's the way he went, over there."

The laborer seemed such an honest simple fellow that at once the nobleman told him how the stranger had swindled his wife.

"Oh, the rogue!" the laborer cried. "To think of his
swindling such a fine lady, too! Master, I wish I
could help you. I'd take that horse of yours and go
after him myself if I could. But I can't. I'm carrying
a bird of great value to a gentleman who lives in the
next town. I have the bird here under my hat and I
daren't leave it."

The nobleman thought that as the laborer had seen
the swindler he might be able to catch him. So he
said:

"My good man, if I sat here and guarded your hat,
would you be willing to mount my horse and follow
that rascal?"

"Indeed I would, my lord, in a minute, for I can't
bear to think of that rogue swindling such a fine
lady as your wife. But I must beg you to be very
careful of this bird. Don't put your hand under my
hat or it might escape and then I should have to bear
the loss of it."

The nobleman promised to be most careful of the
bird and, dismounting, he handed his bridle to the
laborer. That one mounted the nobleman's horse and
galloped off.

It is needless to say the nobleman never saw either
man or horse again. He waited and waited. At last
when he could wait no longer he decided that he
would have to take the bird home with him and let
the laborer follow. So he lifted the edge of the hat

very carefully, slipped in his hand, and clutched--
the dry clod of earth!

Deeply chagrined he went home and had to bear the
smiles of his people as they whispered among
themselves that my lord as well as my lady had
been swindled.

The laborer as he neared his cottage called out to
his wife:

"It's all right, wife! You won't get that beating! I
find that the world is full of people even more
gullible than you!"

THE CANDLES OF LIFE

THE STORY OF A CHILD FOR WHOM DEATH STOOD GODMOTHER

There was once a poor man named Martin. He was so very poor that when his wife gave birth to a little boy, he could find no one who would stand godmother to the child.

"No," he told his wife, "there's no one that I've asked who is willing to hold this infant at the christening."

The poor mother wept and moaned and he tried to comfort her as best he could.

"Don't be discouraged, my dear wife. I promise you your son will be christened. I'll carry him to church myself and if I can find a godmother no other way I'll ask some woman I meet on the road."

So Martin bundled up the baby and carried him to church. On the way he met a woman whom he asked to be godmother. She took the baby in her arms at once and held it during the christening.

Now Martin supposed that she was just an ordinary woman like any other. But she wasn't. She was Death who walks about among men and takes them when their time has come.

After the christening she invited Martin home with her. She showed him through the various rooms of her house and down into great cellars. They went a long way underground through cellar after cellar to a place where thousands upon thousands of candles were burning. There were tall candles just lighted, candles burned halfway down, and little short ones nearly burned out. At one end of the place there was a heap of fresh candles that had not yet been lighted.

"These," Death said, "are the candles of all the people in the world. When a man's candle burns out, then it is time for me to go for him."

"Godmother," Martin said, pointing to a candle that was burning low, "whose may that be?"

"That, my friend, is your candle."

Martin was frightened and begged Death to lengthen his candle, but Death shook her head.

"No, my friend," she said, "I can't do that."

She reached for a fresh candle to light it for the baby just christened. While her back was turned, Martin snatched a tall candle, lighted it, and then pressed it on the stub of his own candle that was nearly burned out.

When Death turned and saw what he had done, she frowned reprovingly.

"That, my friend, was an unworthy trick. However, it has lengthened your life, for what is done is done and can't be undone."

Then she handed Martin some golden ducats as a christening present, took the baby again in her arms, and said:

"Now let us go home and give this young man back to his mother."

At the cottage she made the sick woman comfortable and talked to her about her son. Martin went out to the tavern and bought a jug of ale. Then he spread the table with food, the best he could afford, and Godmother Death sat down on the bench and they ate and drank together.

"Martin," she said to him at last, "you are very poor and I must do something for you. I tell you what I'll do: I'll make you into a great physician. I will spread sickness in the world and you will cure it. Your fame will go abroad and people will send for you and pay you handsomely. This is how we'll work together: when you hear of a person taken sick, go to his house and offer to cure him. I will be there invisible to every one but you. If I stand at the foot of the sick man's bed, you will know that he's going to get well. So then you can prescribe salves and medicines, and when he recovers he'll think you have cured him. But if I stand at the head of the sick man's bed, you will know that he has to die. In that case you must look grave and say that he is beyond help. When he dies people will say how wise you were to know beforehand."

She gave him further instructions and then, after

bidding her godchild and its mother a kind farewell, she left.

Time went by and Martin's fame as a great physician spread far and wide. Wherever Godmother Death caused sickness, there Martin went and made marvelous cures. Dukes and princes heard of him and sent for him. When he rubbed them with salve or gave them a dose or two of bitter medicine and they recovered, they felt so grateful to him that they gave him anything he asked and often more than he asked.

He always remembered Death's warning not to treat a sick man if she stood at his head. Once, however, he disobeyed. He was called to prescribe to a duke of enormous wealth. When he entered the room he saw Death standing at the duke's head.

"Can you cure him?" they asked Martin.

"I can't promise," Martin said, "but I'll do what I can."

He had the servants turn the duke's bed around until the foot instead of the head was in front of Death. The duke recovered and rewarded Martin richly.

But Death when next she met Martin reproved him:

"My friend, don't try that trick on me again. Besides, it is not a real cure. The duke's time has come; he must go to his appointed place; and it is my duty to conduct him thither. You think you have saved him from me and he thinks so, but you are both mistaken. All you have given him is a moment's respite."

The years went by and Martin grew old. His hair whitened and his muscles stiffened. The infirmities of age came upon him and life was no longer a joy.

"Dear Godmother Death," he cried, "I am old and tired! Take me!"

But Death shook her head.

"No, my friend, I can't take you yet. You lengthened the candle of your life and now you must wait until it burns down."

At last one day as he was riding home after visiting a sick man, Death climbed into the carriage with him. She talked with him of old times and they laughed together. Then jokingly she brushed his chin with a green branch. Instantly Martin's eyes grew heavy. His head slipped lower and lower and soon he fell asleep on Death's lap.

"He's dead," the people said, when they looked in the carriage. "The famous Doctor Martin is dead! Oh, what a great and good man he was! Alas, who can take his place!"

He was buried with great pomp and all the world mourned his death.

His son, whose name was Josef, was a stupid fellow. One day as he was going to church, his godmother met him.

"Well, Josef," she asked, "how are you getting on?"

"Oh, pretty well, thank you. I can live along for a while on what my father saved. When that's gone, I don't know what I'll do."

"Tut! Tut!" said Death. "That's no way to talk. If you only knew it, I'm your godmother who held you at your christening. I helped your father to wealth and fame and now I'll help you. I tell you what I'll do: I'll apprentice you to a successful doctor and I'll see to it that soon you'll know more than he knows."

Death rubbed some salve over Josef's ears and led him to a doctor.

"I wish you to take this youth as an apprentice," she said. "He's a likely lad and will do you credit. Teach him all you know."

The doctor accepted Josef as an apprentice and when he went out into the fields to gather herbs and simples, he took the youth with him.

Now the magic salve with which Godmother Death had anointed Josef enabled him to hear and understand the whisperings of the herbs. Each one as he picked it, whispered to him its secret properties.

"I cure a fever," one whispered.

"And I a rash."

"And I a boil."

The doctor was amazed at his apprentice's knowledge of herbs.

"You know them better than I do," he said. "You never make a mistake. It is I should be apprentice, not you. Let us go into partnership. I will work under you and together we will make wonderful cures."

And so, owing to his godmother's gift, Josef became a great physician of whom it was said that there was no illness for which he could not find a remedial herb.

He lived long and happily until at last his candle burned down and Death, his kind godmother, took him.

THE DEVIL'S GIFTS

THE STORY OF A MAN WHOM THE DEVIL BEFRIENDED

There were once two men, a shoemaker and a farmer, who had been close friends in youth. The shoemaker married and had many children to whom the farmer stood godfather. For this reason the two men called each other "Godfather." When they met it was "Godfather, this," and "Godfather, that." The shoemaker was an industrious little man and yet with so many mouths to fill he remained poor. The farmer on the other hand soon grew rich for he had no children to eat into his savings.

Years went by and money and possessions began to change the farmer's disposition. The more he accumulated, the more he wanted, until people were whispering behind his back that he was miserly and avaricious. His wife was like him. She, too, saved and skimped although, as I have told you, they had neither chick nor child to provide for.

The richer the farmer grew, the less he cared for his poor friend and his poor friend's children. Now when they called him "Godfather," he frowned impatiently, and whenever he saw any of them he pretended to be very busy for fear they should ask him a favor.

One day when he had slaughtered beef, the poor shoemaker came to him and said:

"My dear Godfather, you have just made a killing.

Won't you please give me a little piece of meat? My wife and children are hungry."

"No!" roared the rich man. "Why should I feed your family? You ought to save as I do and then you wouldn't have to ask favors of any one."

Humiliated by the refusal, the shoemaker went home and told his wife what his friend had said.

"Go back to him," his wife insisted, "and tell him again that his godchildren are hungry. I don't think he understood you."

So the poor little shoemaker returned to the rich man. He cleared his throat apologetically and stammered:

"Dear Godfather, you--you don't want your poor godchildren to go hungry, do you? Give me just one small piece of meat--that's all I ask."

In a rage, the rich man picked up a hunk of meat and threw it at his poor friend.

"There!" he shouted. "And now go to hell, you and the meat with you, and tell the Devil I sent you."

The shoemaker picked up the piece of meat. It was all fat and gristle.

"No use carrying this home," he thought to himself. "I think I better do as Godfather says. Yes, I'll go to hell and give it to the Devil."

So he tramped down to hell and presented himself
at the gate. The little devil who stood on guard
greeted him merrily.

"Hello, shoemaker! What do you want here?"

"I have a present for the Devil, a piece of meat that
Godfather gave me."

The little devil of a guard nodded his head
understandingly.

"I see, I see. Very well then, come with me and I'll
lead you to Prince Lucifer. But I'll give you a bit of
advice first. When the Prince asks you what present
you'd like in return, tell him you'd like the
tablecloth off his own table."

The little devil of a guard then conducted the
shoemaker into Prince Lucifer's presence and the
Prince received him with every mark of
consideration. The shoemaker told him what
Godfather had said and presented him the hunk of
meat. Lucifer received it most graciously. Then he
said:

"Now, my dear shoemaker, let me make you a little
present in return. Do you see anything here that
you'd like?"

"If it pleases your Highness," the shoemaker said,
"give me that cloth that is spread over your table."

Lucifer at once handed him the cloth and dismissed

him with many wishes for a pleasant journey back to earth.

As the shoemaker was leaving the friendly little devil of a guard said to him:

"I just want to tell you that's no ordinary tablecloth that the Prince has given you. No, indeed! Whenever you're hungry, all you've got to do is spread out that cloth and say: 'Meat and drink for one!' or, for as many as you want, and instantly you will have what you ask."

Overjoyed at his good fortune the little shoemaker hurried back to earth. As night came on he stopped at a tavern. He thought this was a good place to try the tablecloth. So he took it out of his bag, spread it over the table, and said:

"Meat and drink for one!"

Instantly a fine supper appeared and the shoemaker ate and drank his fill.

Now the landlord of the tavern was an evil, covetous fellow and when he saw how the tablecloth worked his fingers itched to own it. He called his wife aside and told her in guarded whispers what he had seen.

Her eyes, too, filled with greed.

"Husband," she whispered back, "we've got to get possession of that tablecloth! Think what a help it

would be to us in our business! I tell you what we'll
do: tonight when the shoemaker is asleep we'll steal
his tablecloth and slip in one of our own in its place.
He's a simple fellow and will never know the
difference."

So that night while the shoemaker was asleep, they
tip-toed in, stole the magic tablecloth out of the bag,
and substituted one of their own.

The next morning when the shoemaker awoke and
spread out the cloth which he found in his bag and
said: "Meat and drink for one!" of course nothing
happened.

"That's strange," he thought to himself. "I'll have to
take this back to the Devil and ask him to give me
something else."

So instead of going home he went back to hell and
knocked at the gate.

"Hello, shoemaker!" the little devil of a guard said.
"What do you want now?"

"Well, you see it's this way," the shoemaker
explained: "this tablecloth of the Devil's worked all
right last night but it doesn't work this morning."

The little devil grinned.

"Oh, I see. And you want Prince Lucifer to take it
back and give you something else, eh? Well, I'm
sure he will. If you want my advice, I should say to

ask him for that red rooster that sits in the chimney corner."

The Prince received the shoemaker as kindly as before and was perfectly willing to exchange the tablecloth for the red rooster.

When the shoemaker got back to the gate, the little devil of a guard said:

"I see you've got the red rooster. Now I just want to tell you that's no ordinary rooster. Whenever you need money, all you have to do is put that rooster on the table and say: 'Crow, rooster, crow!' He'll crow and as he crows a golden ducat will drop from his bill!"

"What a lucky fellow I am!" the little shoemaker thought to himself as he hurried back to earth.

As night came on he stopped again at the same tavern and, when it was time to pay for his supper, he put the red rooster on the table and said:

"Crow, rooster, crow!"

The rooster crowed and sure enough a golden ducat dropped from his bill.

The covetous landlord licked his greedy lips and hurried off to his wife.

"We've got a red rooster," the wife said. "I'll tell you what we'll do: when the shoemaker's asleep

we'll trade roosters. He's a simple fellow and will
never know the difference."

So the next morning after breakfast, when the
shoemaker put what he thought was his own rooster
on the table and said: "Crow, rooster, crow!" of
course nothing happened.

"I wonder what's the matter with you," he said to
the rooster. "I'll have to take you back to the Devil."

So again he tramped down to hell and explained to
the little devil of a guard that the rooster no longer
dropped golden ducats from his bill.

The little devil listened and grinned.

"I suppose you want Prince Lucifer to give you
something else, eh?"

The shoemaker nodded.

"I'm sure he will," the little devil said. "He seems to
have taken quite a fancy to you. Now take my
advice and ask him for the pair of clubs that are
lying under the oven."

So the shoemaker when he was led again into
Lucifer's presence explained to the Prince that the
red rooster no longer worked and please would His
Highness give him something else instead.

The Prince was most affable.

"Certainly," he said.

"Well then, Your Highness, I'd like that pair of clubs I see under the oven."

Lucifer gave him the clubs and wished him a pleasant journey home.

When the shoemaker got back to the gate, the little devil of a guard wagged his head and blinked his eyes.

"Shoemaker," he said, "those are fine clubs! You don't know how fine they are! Why, they'll do anything you tell them! If you point to a man and say to them: 'Tickle that fellow!' they'll jump about and tickle him under the ribs. If you say: 'Strike that fellow!' they'll hit him. And if you say: 'Beat him!' they'll give him a terrible drubbing. Now I want you to try these clubs on that landlord and his wife for they have been playing tricks on you. They stole your tablecloth and your rooster. When you reach the tavern tonight, they'll be entertaining a wedding party and they'll say they haven't any room for you. Don't argue but quietly take out your clubs and order them to knock about among the wedding guests. Then order them to beat the landlord and his wife and those two will soon cry for mercy and be more than willing to return you your property."

The shoemaker thanked the little devil of a guard for his good advice and, putting the clubs in his bag, climbed back to earth. When he reached the tavern, sure enough he found a wedding party feasting and dancing.

"Get out of here!" the landlord cried. "There's no room for you!"

Without a word the shoemaker took out his clubs and said:

"Clubs, knock around among the wedding guests!"

Instantly the two clubs went knocking about among the wedding guests, tickling some and throwing down others, until the place was in an uproar.

"Now beat the landlord and his wife!" the shoemaker cried.

At that the clubs hopped over to the landlord and his wife and began beating them over the head and shoulders until they both dropped on their knees before the shoemaker and begged for mercy.

"Are you ready to give me back my tablecloth and rooster?" the shoemaker asked.

"Yes, yes!" they cried. "Only call off your clubs and we'll give you back your tablecloth and rooster--we swear we will!"

When he thought he had punished them enough, the shoemaker ordered the clubs to stop and the landlord and his wife tottered off as fast as their trembling legs could carry them. Presently they returned with the tablecloth and the rooster.

So the shoemaker, when he got home, had all three

of the Devil's presents tucked safely away in his bag.

"Now, wife!" he cried. "Now, children! Now we are going to have a feast!"

He spread out the tablecloth and said:

"Meat and drink for ten!"

Instantly such a feast appeared that for a moment the poor wife and the hungry children couldn't believe their eyes. Then they set to, and, oh! I can't begin to tell you all they ate!

When they could eat no more, the shoemaker said:

"That isn't all. I've got something else in my bag."

He took out the clubs and said:

"Clubs, tickle the children!"

Instantly the clubs hopped around among the children and tickled them under the ribs until they were all roaring with laughter.

"And that isn't all!" the shoemaker said. "I've got something else in my bag."

He pulled out the red rooster, put him on the table, and said:

"Crow, rooster, crow!"

The rooster crowed and a golden ducat dropped from his bill.

"Oh!" the children cried, and the youngest one begged: "Make him do it again! Make him do it again!"

So again the shoemaker said: "Crow, rooster, crow!" and again a golden ducat dropped from the rooster's bill.

The children were so amused that the shoemaker kept the rooster crowing all night long until the room was overflowing with a great heap of shining ducats.

The next day the shoemaker said to his wife:

"We must measure our money and see how much we have. Send one of the children over to Godfather to borrow a bushel measure."

So the youngest child ran over to the rich man's house and said:

"Godfather, my father says will you please lend us a bushel measure to measure our money."

"Measure your money!" the rich man growled. "Pooh, pooh, what nonsense! Wife, where's that old worn-out measure that we're going to throw away? It's the very thing to lend these beggars."

The woman who was just as disagreeable as the

man handed the child an old broken measure and said, severely:

"See you bring it back at once!"

In a short time the little girl returned the measure.

"Thanks, Godfather," she said. "We've got a hundred bushels."

"A hundred bushels!" the farmer repeated scornfully after the child was gone. "A hundred bushels of what? Look inside the measure, wife, and see if you find a trace of anything."

The woman peered inside the measure and found a golden ducat lodged in a slit. She took it out and the mere sight of it made her face and her husband's face turn sick and pale with envy.

"Do you suppose those beggars really have got some money?" he said. "We better go over at once and see."

So they hurried over to the shoemaker's cottage and they shook hands with him and his wife most effusively and they rubbed their hands together and they smiled and they smiled and the rich man said:

"Dear Godfather, how are you? And how are all my dear godchildren? And what is this good fortune that has come to you?"

"I owe it all to you," the shoemaker said.

"To me?" the farmer repeated and, although he began to feel sick inside to think that any one had benefited through him, he kept on smiling and rubbing his hands. "Tell me about it, dear Godfather."

"You know that piece of meat you gave me," the shoemaker said. "You told me to give it to the Devil. I took your advice and made the Devil a present of it and he gave me all these wonderful things in return."

The shoemaker made the tablecloth spread itself, he made the rooster crow and drop a golden ducat, and he made the clubs dance merrily around the room and tickle the children under the ribs.

The farmer and his wife grew sicker and sicker with envy but they kept on smiling and rubbing their hands and asking questions.

"Tell us, dear Godfather," they said, "what road do you take to go to hell? Of course we're not expecting to go ourselves but we'd just like to know."

The shoemaker told them the way and they hurried home. They slaughtered their finest cattle and then, packing on their backs all the choicest cuts of the meat, they staggered down to hell.

When the little devil of a guard saw them coming, he grinned and chuckled.

"Welcome!" he cried. "We've been waiting for you

a long time! Come right in!"

He led them to Prince Lucifer and the Prince
recognized them instantly.

"It's very good of you coming before you had to,"
he said. "This saves me a trip to earth. I was
thinking just the other day it was time to go after
you. And see all that fine meat you've brought with
you! I certainly am glad to see you! It isn't often I
have the pleasure of meeting people as avaricious,
as greedy, as mean, as you two have been. In fact,
both of you are such ornaments to hell that I think
I'll just have to keep you here forever!"

So the rich farmer and his wife were never again
seen on earth.

As for the shoemaker--he and his family lived long
and merrily. They shared their good fortune with
others, never forgetting the time when they, too,
suffered from poverty. And because they were good
and kind, the Devil's gifts brought them only
happiness.

GENTLE DORA

THE STORY OF A DEVIL WHO MARRIED A SCOLD

There was once a young devil who, as he wandered over the earth, found a book. He slipped it carelessly into his pocket and carried it down to hell. Now this book contained a list of the good deeds of a rich man, and the account of a good deed is of course never allowed to enter hell.

The devils in hell when they opened the book were greatly incensed over their comrade's stupidity and at once they dragged him off to Prince Lucifer for punishment.

Lucifer when he heard the case shook his head gravely.

"This is a serious offense," he said to the culprit. "To atone you must do one of two things: every day for seven years you must bring a soul to hell, or you must remain on earth for seven years and take service among men. Which will you do?"

The young devil was a stupid fellow and he knew he would never be able to seduce a soul every day for seven years. So he said:

"If I must choose, Your Majesty, let it be exile on earth for seven years."

So Lucifer pronounced sentence and the young

devil was driven out of hell and warned not to
return until the seven years were up.

Sad and forlorn he wandered up and down the
world looking for work. People everywhere were
suspicious of his black face and turned him away.

One day he met a man to whom he told his story.

"And just because I'm a devil," he said in
conclusion, "no one will hire me."

"I know where you can get work," the man told
him. "Just beyond the next village there is a big
farm which is owned by a woman. She's always in
need of laborers for she has such a sharp tongue and
such a mean disposition that no one can stay with
her longer than a month. Her name is Dora and in
mockery the people hereabouts call her Gentle
Dora. Why don't you take service with her? As
you're a devil, you may be able to get the best of
her."

The devil thanked the man for this suggestion and at
once presented himself to Gentle Dora. Gentle
Dora, as usual, was in need of laborers and so she
employed the devil instantly in spite of his black
face.

From the start she worked him like a slave from
morning till night, scolded him incessantly, and
didn't give him half enough to eat. The poor fellow
grew thin and almost pale. The months went by and
each new month was harder to live through than the
one before.

"I can do a day's work with the best of them," the devil thought to himself, "but there is no one, either man or devil, who can stand this woman's everlasting nagging. Oh dear, oh dear, what shall I do?"

Now Gentle Dora was looking for a husband. She had already had five husbands all of whom she had nagged to death. On account of this record every bachelor and widower in the village was a little shy of proposing himself as a sixth husband.

The devil, who as I have told you was a simple fellow, finally decided that it would be a mighty clever thing for him to marry Gentle Dora. He felt sure that once he was her husband she would give him less work and more food. So he proposed to her.

The rich widow didn't much fancy his black face, but on the other hand she wanted a husband and so, as there was no other prospect in sight, she accepted him.

"At least," she thought to herself, "by making him my husband, I'll save his wages."

It wasn't long before the devil found out that life as a husband was even harder than life as a laborer. Now without wages he had ten times more to do while Gentle Dora did nothing but spend her time hunting work for him.

"Why do you think I've married," she would cry, "if it isn't to have some one take care of me!"

So she would stand over him and scold and scold and scold while he, poor devil, toiled and sweated, doing the work of six men.

Time went by and the devil grew thinner and thinner and paler and paler. Gentle Dora begrudged him every mouthful he ate and was forever harping on his enormous appetite.

At last one day she said to him:

"You're simply eating me out of house and home. From now on you will have to board yourself. As I'm an honest woman I'll treat you justly. This year we'll divide the harvest half and half. Which will you have: that which grows above the ground, or that which grows below the ground?"

This sounded fair enough and the devil said:

"Give me the part that grows above the ground."

Thereupon Gentle Dora had the whole farm planted in potatoes and beets and carrots. When the harvest came she gave the devil the tops and herself took all the tubers.

That winter the poor devil would have starved if the neighbors hadn't taken pity on him and fed him.

In the spring Gentle Dora asked him what part of the new crop he wanted.

"This time," he said, "give me the part that grows

under the ground."

Gentle Dora agreed and then planted the entire farm in millet and rye and poppy seed. At the harvest she took all the grain as her share and told the devil that the worthless roots belonged to him.

"What chance has a poor devil with such a woman?" he thought to himself bitterly.

Discouraged and unhappy he went out to the roadside where he sat down. The troubles of domestic life pressed upon him so heavily that soon he began to cry.

Presently a journeyman shoemaker came by and said to him:

"Comrade, what ails you?"

The devil looked at the shoemaker and, when he saw that the shoemaker was a friendly sort of person, he told him his story.

"Why do you stand such treatment?" the shoemaker asked.

The devil snuffled.

"How can I help it? I'm married to her."

"How can you help it?" the shoemaker repeated. "Comrade, look at me. At home I have just such a wife as your Gentle Dora. There was no living with

her in peace, so one morning bright and early I ups
and puts my tool kit on my shoulder and leaves her.
Now I wander about from place to place, mending a
shoe here and a slipper there, and life is much
pleasanter than it used to be. Why don't you leave
your Gentle Dora and come along with me? We'll
make out somehow."

The devil was overjoyed at the suggestion and
without a moment's hesitation he tramped off with
the shoemaker.

"You won't regret the kindness you've done me,"
the devil said. "I'm so thin and pale that probably
you don't realize I'm a devil. But I am and I can
reward you."

They wandered about together for a long time living
on the shoemaker's earnings. At last one day the
devil said:

"Comrade, you have befriended me long enough. It
is now my turn to do something for you. I've got a
fine idea. You see that big town we're coming to?
Well, I'll hurry on ahead and take possession of the
prince's young daughter. You come along more
slowly and when you hear the proclamation that the
prince will richly reward any one who will cure his
daughter, present yourself at the palace. When they
lead you to the princess, make mysterious passes
over her and mumble some gibberish. Then I will
quit her body and the prince will reward you."

The devil's scheme worked perfectly. When the
shoemaker reached the town the herald was already

proclaiming the sad news that the princess had been taken possession of by a devil and that the prince was in search of a capable exorcist.

The shoemaker presented himself at the palace, made mysterious passes over the princess's body, pretended to mumble magic incantations, and in a short time had apparently succeeded in exorcising the devil.

In his gratitude for the princess's recovery, the prince paid the shoemaker a hundred golden ducats.

The devil waited for the shoemaker outside the town gate.

"You see," he said when the shoemaker had shown him the money, "I'm not an ungrateful devil."

They turned the same trick in several other cities until the shoemaker had a heavy bag of gold.

"Now you're a rich man," the devil said, "and we can part company. My seven years are up and I am going soon to return to hell. But before I go I'm going to take possession of one more princess. I served Gentle Dora so long that it's a pleasant change to rule some one. This time don't you try to exorcise me. You're famous now and the princess's father will probably hunt you out and beg you to cure his daughter, but you must excuse yourself. This is all I ask of you. If you allow yourself to be persuaded, I'll punish you by taking possession of your body. Don't forget!"

They bade each other good-bye and parted, the shoemaker going west and the devil east.

Soon word began to pass up and down the land that there was a great king toward the east who needed the services of the famous exorcist to restore his daughter. Emissaries of the king found the shoemaker and against his will dragged him to court. He declared he was powerless to help the princess but the king wouldn't listen to him and threatened him with torture and death if he refused to make the effort.

"Well then," the shoemaker said, after much thought, "chain the princess to her bed, order out all the attendants, and let me see her alone."

The king had these conditions fulfilled and the shoemaker went boldly into the princess's chamber.

"Hist! Devil!" he called softly.

Instantly the devil jumped out of the princess's mouth and when he saw the shoemaker he stamped his foot in anger.

"What!" he cried. "You've come after my warning! Don't you remember what I told you?"

The shoemaker put his finger to his lips and winked.

"Softly, comrade," he whispered, "softly! I'm not come to exorcise you but to warn you. You know that precious wife of yours, Gentle Dora? Well, she's traced you here and she's down in the courtyard now waiting for you."

The devil turned white with fright.

"Gentle Dora!" he gasped. "Lucifer, help me!"

Without another word he jumped out the window and flew straight down to hell as fast as the wind could carry him. And so great is his fear of Gentle Dora that he has never dared to show his face on earth again.

The king rewarded the shoemaker royally and to this day the shoemaker is wandering merrily about from place to place. Whenever he hears of a woman who is a scold, he says:

"Why, she's a regular Gentle Dora, isn't she?"

And when people ask him: "Who's Gentle Dora?" he tells them this story.

THE DEVIL'S MATCH

THE STORY OF A FARMER WHO
REMEMBERED WHAT HIS GRANDMOTHER
TOLD HIM

Once upon a time there was a poor farmer who
lived in a wretched tumble-down cottage beyond
the village and whose farm consisted of a miserable
little field no bigger than your hand. His children
were ragged and hungry and his wife was always
worried over getting them enough to eat.

Yet the farmer was a clever fellow with a quick
shrewd wit and people used to say that he'd be able
to fool the devil if ever he had the chance. One day
the chance came.

His wife had sent him into the forest to gather a
bundle of faggots. Suddenly without any warning a
young man with black face and shiny eyes stood
before him.

"It's a devil, of course," the farmer told himself.
"But even so there's no use being frightened."

So he wished the devil a civil good-day and the
devil, who was really a very simple fellow indeed,
returned his greeting and asked him what he was
doing in the forest.

Now the farmer suddenly remembered that his
grandmother had once told him devils were afraid
of lime trees because the bast from lime trees is the
one thing in the world they are unable to break.

That's why, when you catch a devil, you must tie his hands together with bast.

So the farmer, recalling what his grandmother had said, remarked casually:

"Oh, I'm looking for a lime tree. I want to strip off some bast. Then I'm going after them"--and when he said them he paused significantly--"and tie them hand and foot."

He peeped at the devil out of the corner of his eye and saw that the devil had turned almost white under his black skin.

"He is a foolish one!" he thought to himself.

"Oh, don't do that!" the devil cried. "What have we ever done to you?"

The farmer pretended to be firm and repeated that that was just what he was going to do.

"Please listen to me," the devil begged. "If you promise to let us alone I tell you what I'll do: I'll bring you such a big bag of gold that it will make you a rich man."

At first the farmer, being a shrewd fellow, pretended that he cared nothing for money. Then gradually he let himself be persuaded and at last said:

"Very well. If you bring me the gold within an hour

I won't bind you with bast. But don't keep me waiting or I may change my mind."

The young devil--oh, you never saw a more stupid young fellow!--scurried off and, long before the hour was up, he came panting back with a great big bag of gold.

"Is that enough?" he asked.

The farmer who had really never seen so much money in all his life hemmed and hawed but finally said:

"Well, it isn't as much as I expected but I'll accept it."

The young devil, delighted with his bargain, hurried back to hell and told all his black comrades how grateful they ought to be to him for saving them from the farmer who was planning to bind them, hand and foot, with bast.

When the other devils heard the whole story, they laughed at him loud and long.

"You are certainly the stupidest devil in hell!" they said. "Why, that man has made a fool of you!"

They discussed the matter among themselves and decided that the devil would have to get back the bag of gold or the story would leak out and thereafter the people on earth would have no more respect for devils.

"Go back to the farmer," they said, "and dare him to a wrestling match. Tell him that whoever wins the match is to keep the gold."

So the young devil went back to earth and dared the farmer to a wrestling match. The farmer, who saw how things were, said:

"My dear young friend, if I were to wrestle with you I'm afraid I'd hurt you for I'm awfully strong. I tell you what I'll do: I'll let you wrestle with my old grandfather. He's ninety-nine years old but even so he's more nearly in your class."

The devil agreed to this and the farmer--oh, but that farmer was a sly one!--led him out into the forest to a cave where a big brown bear lay asleep.

"There's my grandfather," the farmer said. "Go wake him up and make him wrestle."

The devil shook the bear and said:

"Wake up, old man! Wake up! We're going to wrestle!"

The bear opened his little eyes, stood up on his hind legs, and taking the devil in his arms hugged him until the devil thought his bones would all be crushed. It was as much as the devil could do to escape with his life.

"Oh, my poor ribs! My poor ribs!" he gasped when he was safely back in hell. "He's a terrible man--that farmer! Why, even his old grandfather is so strong that I thought he'd squeeze me to death!"

But when he had told his full story the other devils laughed at him louder than before and told him that the farmer had again fooled him.

"You've got to try another match with him," they said. "This time dare him to a foot race and mind you don't let him fool you."

So in a day or two when the soreness was gone from his bones the devil went back to earth and dared the farmer to run a foot race with him.

"Certainly," the farmer said, "but it's hardly fair to let you run against me because I go like the wind. I tell you what I'll do: I'll let you race with my small son. He's only a year old and perhaps you can beat him."

The devil--I never knew a more stupid fellow in my life!--agreed to this and the farmer took him out to a meadow. Under some bushes he showed him a rabbit's hole.

"My little boy's asleep in there," he said. "Call him out."

"Little boy!" the devil called. "Come out and run a race with me!"

Instantly a rabbit jumped out of the hole and went hoppetylop across the meadow. The devil tried hard

to overtake him but couldn't. He ran on and on.
They came at last to a deep ravine. The rabbit
leaped across but the devil, when he tried to do the
same, slipped and fell and went rolling down over
stones and brambles, down, down, down, into a
brook. When he had dragged himself out of the
water, bruised and scratched, the rabbit had
disappeared.

"I've had enough of that farmer," the devil said
when he got back to hell. "Why, do you know, he
has a small boy just one year old and I tell you there
isn't one of you can beat that boy running!"

But the devils when they heard the rest of the story
only laughed and jeered and told their comrade that
the farmer had again tricked him.

"You've got to go back to him another time," they
said. "It will never do for people to get the idea that
devils are such fools."

"But I tell you I won't dare him to another wrestling
match," the young devil said, "nor to a foot race,
either."

"Try whistling this time," his comrades told him.
"You ought to be able to beat him whistling. Now
have your wits about you and don't let him fool you
again."

So the devil went back to earth and said to the
farmer:

"We've got to have another contest for that bag of

money. This time let's try whistling."

"Very well," the farmer said. "We'll have a whistling match."

They went off into the forest and the farmer told the devil to whistle first.

The devil whistled and all the leaves on the trees shook and trembled. He whistled again and the twigs began to crackle and break. He whistled a third time and big branches snapped off and fell to the ground.

"There!" the devil exclaimed, "Can you beat that?"

"My poor boy," the farmer said. (Oh, but that farmer was a tricky one!) "Is that the best you can do? Why, when I whistle, if you don't cover up your ears you'll be deafened! And as likely as not a tree will fall on you and kill you! Now shall I begin?"

"Wait a minute!" the devil begged. "Won't you please tie up my ears before you begin because I don't want to be deafened."

This was just what the farmer was hoping the devil would say. So he took out a big kerchief and put it over the devil's ears and also over his eyes and tied it behind in a hard knot.

"Now then!" he shouted. "Take care!"

With that he began to whistle and as he whistled he

picked up a big branch off the ground and gave the devil an awful crack over the head.

"My head! My head!" the devil cried.

"My poor fellow!" the farmer said, pretending to be very sympathetic. "I hope that tree as it fell down didn't hurt you! Now I'm going to whistle again and you must be more careful."

This time when he whistled the farmer struck the devil over the head harder than before.

"That's enough!" the devil shouted. "Another tree has fallen on me! Stop! Stop!"

"No," the farmer insisted. "You whistled three times and I'm going to whistle three times. Are you ready?"

The poor devil had to say: "Yes," and thereupon the farmer began to whistle and at the same time to beat the devil over his head and shoulders until the devil supposed that the whole forest was falling on him.

"Stop whistling!" he shouted. "Stop or I'll be killed!"

But the farmer wouldn't stop until he was too exhausted to beat the devil any longer.

Then he paused and asked:

"Shall I whistle some more?"

"No! No! No!" the devil roared. "Undo the kerchief and let me go and I swear I'll never come back!"

So the farmer undid the kerchief and the devil fled, too terrified to stop even long enough to look around for all those fallen trees.

He never came back and the farmer was left in undisputed possession of the gold.

"I owe all my good fortune to my old grandmother," the farmer used to say, "for she it was who told me to tie them with bast."

THE DEVIL'S LITTLE BROTHER-IN-LAW

THE STORY OF A YOUTH WHO COULDN'T FIND WORK

Once upon a time there was a youth named Peter. He was the son of a rich farmer but on his father's death his stepmother robbed him of his inheritance and drove him out into the world, penniless and destitute.

"Begone with you now!" she shouted. "Never let me see your face again!"

"Where shall I go?" Peter asked.

"Go to the Devil, for all I care!" the stepmother cried and slammed the door in his face.

Peter felt very sad at being driven away from the farm that had always been his home, but he was an able-bodied lad, industrious and energetic, and he thought he would have no trouble making his way in the world.

He tramped to the next village and stopped at a big farmhouse. The farmer was standing at the door, eating a great hunk of buttered bread.

Peter touched his hat respectfully and said:

"Let every one praise Lord Jesus!"

With his mouth stuffed full, the farmer responded:

"Until the Day of Judgment!" Then in a different tone he demanded: "What do you want?"

"I'm looking for work," Peter said. "Do you need a laborer?"

Peter was well dressed for he had on the last clothes his kind father had given him. The farmer looked him over and sneered.

"A fine laborer you would make! You would do good work at meals--I see that, and spend the rest of your time at cards and teasing the maids! I know your kind!"

Peter tried to tell the farmer that he was industrious and steady but with an oath the farmer told him to go to the Devil. Then stepping inside the house he slammed the door in Peter's face.

In the next village he applied for work at the bailiff's house. The bailiff's wife answered his knock.

"The master is playing cards with two of his friends," she said. "I'll go in and ask him if he has anything for you to do."

Peter heard her speak to some one inside and then a rough voice bellowed out:

"No! How often have I told you not to interrupt me when I'm busy! Tell the fellow to go to the Devil!"

Without waiting for the bailiff's wife, Peter turned away. Tired and discouraged he took a path into the woods and sat down.

"There doesn't seem to be any place for me in all the world," he thought to himself. "They all tell me to go to the Devil--my stepmother, the farmer, and now the bailiff. If I knew the way to hell I think I'd take their advice. I'm sure the Devil would treat me better than they do!"

Just then a handsome gentleman, dressed in green, walked by. Peter touched his hat politely and said:

"Let every one praise Lord Jesus."

The man passed him without responding. Then he looked back and asked Peter why he looked so discouraged.

"I have reason to look discouraged," Peter said. "Everywhere I ask for work they tell me to go to the Devil. If I knew the way to hell I think I'd take their advice and go."

The stranger smiled.

"But if you saw the Devil, don't you think you'd be afraid of him?"

Peter shook his head.

"He can't be any worse than my stepmother, or the farmer, or the bailiff."

The man suddenly turned black.

"Look at me!" he cried. "Here I am, the very person we've been talking about!"

With no show of fear Peter looked the Devil up and down.

Then the Devil said that if Peter still wished to enter his service, he would take him. The work would be light, the Devil said, and the hours good, and if Peter did as he was told he would have a pleasant time. The Devil promised to keep him seven years and at the end of that time to make him a handsome present and set him free.

Peter shook hands on the bargain and the Devil, taking him about the waist, whisked him up into the air, and, pst! before Peter knew what was happening, they were in hell.

The Devil gave Peter a leather apron and led him into a room where there were three big cauldrons.

"Now it's your duty," the Devil said, "to keep the fires under these cauldrons always burning. Keep four logs under the first cauldron, eight logs under the second, and twelve under the third. Be careful never to let the fires go out. And another thing, Peter: you're never to peep inside the cauldrons. If you do I'll drive you away without a cent of wages. Don't forget!"

So Peter began working for the Devil and the treatment he received was so much better than that

which he had had on earth that, sometimes, it
seemed to him he was in heaven rather than hell. He
had plenty of good food and drink and, as the Devil
had promised him, the work was not heavy.

For companions he had the young apprentice devils,
a merry black crew, who told droll stories and
played amusing pranks.

Time passed quickly. Peter was faithful at his work
and never once peeped under the lids of his three
cauldrons.

At last he began to grow homesick for the world
and one day he asked the Devil how much longer he
had still to serve.

"Tomorrow," the Devil told him, "your seven years
are up."

The next day while Peter was piling fresh logs
under the cauldrons, the Devil came to him and
said:

"Today, Peter, you are free. You have served me
faithfully and well and I am going to reward you
handsomely. Money would be too heavy for you to
carry, so I am going to give you this bag which is a
magic bag. Whenever you open it and say: 'Bag, I
need some ducats,' the bag will always have just as
many as you need. Good luck go with you, Peter.
However, I don't believe you'll have a very good
time at first for people will think you're a devil. You
know you do look pretty black for you haven't
washed for seven years and you haven't cut your

hair or nails."

"That's true," said Peter. "I just remember I haven't washed ever since I've been down here. I certainly must take a bath and get my hair cut and my nails trimmed."

The Devil shook his head.

"No, Peter, one bath won't do it. Water won't wash off the kind of black you get down here. I know what you must do but I won't tell you just yet. Go up into the world as you are and, if ever you need me, call me. If the people up there ask you who you are, tell them you're the Devil's little brother-in-law. This isn't a joke. It's true as you'll find out some day."

Peter then took leave of all the little black apprentices and the Devil, lifting him on his back, whisked him up to earth and set him down in the forest on exactly the same spot where they had met seven years before.

The Devil disappeared and Peter, stuffing the magic bag in his pocket, walked to the nearest village.

His appearance created a panic. On sight of him the children ran screaming home, crying out:

"The Devil! The Devil is coming!"

Mothers and fathers ran out of the houses to see what was the matter but on sight of Peter they ran in

again, barred all the doors and windows, and
making the sign of the cross prayed God Almighty
to protect them.

Peter went on to the tavern. The landlord and his
wife were standing in the doorway. As Peter came
toward them, they cried out in fright:

"O Lord, forgive us our sins! The Devil is coming!"

They tried to run away but they tripped over each
other and fell down, and before they could scramble
to their feet Peter stood before them.

He looked at them for a moment and laughed. Then
he went inside the tavern, sat down, and said:

"Landlord, bring me a drink!"

Quaking with fright the landlord went to the cellar
and drew a pitcher of beer. Then he called the little
herd who was working in the stable.

"Yirik," he said to the boy, "take this beer into the
house. There's a man in there waiting for it. He's a
little strange looking but you needn't be afraid. He
won't hurt you."

Yirik took the pitcher of beer and started in. He
opened the door and then, as he caught sight of
Peter, he dropped the pitcher and fled.

The landlord scolded him angrily.

"What do you mean," he shouted, "not giving the gentleman his beer? And breaking the pitcher, too! The price of it will be deducted from your wages! Draw another pitcher of beer and place it at once before the gentleman."

Yirik feared Peter but he feared the landlord more. He was an orphan, poor lad, and served the landlord for his keep and three dollars a year.

So with trembling fingers he drew a pitcher of beer and then, breathing a prayer to his patron saint, he slowly dragged himself into the tavern.

"There, there, boy," Peter called out kindly. "You needn't be afraid. I'm not going to hurt you. I'm not the Devil. I'm only his little brother-in-law."

Yirik took heart and placed the beer in front of Peter. Then he stood still, not daring to raise his eyes.

Peter began asking him about himself, who he was, how he came to be working for the landlord, and what kind of treatment he was receiving. Yirik stammered out his story and as he talked he forgot his fear, he forgot that Peter looked like a devil, and presently he was talking to him freely as one friend to another.

Peter was touched by the orphan's story and, pulling out his magic money bag, he filled Yirik's cap with golden ducats. The boy danced about the room with delight. Then he ran outside and showed the landlord and the people who had gathered the present which the strange gentleman had made him.

"And he says he's not the Devil," Yirik reported,
"but only his brother-in-law."

When the landlord heard that Peter really hadn't any
horns or a flaming tongue, he picked up courage
and going inside he begged Peter to give him, too, a
few golden ducats. But Peter only laughed at him.

Peter stayed at the tavern overnight. Just as he fell
asleep some one shook his hand and, as he opened
his eyes, he saw his old master standing beside him.

"Quick!" the Devil whispered. "Get up and hurry
out to the shed! The landlord is about to murder the
orphan for his money."

Peter jumped out of bed and ran outside to the shed
where Yirik slept. He burst open the door just as the
landlord was ready to stab the sleeping boy with a
dagger.

"You sinner!" Peter cried. "I've caught you at last!
Off to hell you go with me this instant to stew
forever in boiling oil!"

The landlord fainted with terror. Peter dragged him
senseless into the house. When he came to himself
he fell on his knees before Peter and begged for
mercy. He offered Peter everything he possessed if
only Peter would grant him another chance and he
solemnly vowed that he would repent and give up
his evil ways.

At last Peter said:

"Very well. I'll give you another chance provided that, from this time on, you treat Yirik as your son. Be kind to him and send him to school. The moment you forget your promise and treat him cruelly, I'll come and carry you off to hell! Remember!"

There was no need to urge the landlord to remember. From that night he was a changed man. He became honest in all his dealings and he really did treat Yirik as though he were his own son.

Peter stayed on at the tavern and stories about him and his golden ducats began to spread through the country-side. The prince of the land heard of him and sent word that he would like to see him at the castle. Peter answered the prince's messenger that if the prince wished to see him he could come to the tavern.

"Who is this prince of yours," Peter asked the landlord, "and why does he want to see me?"

"He'd probably like to borrow some money from you," the landlord said. "He's deep in debt for he has two of the wickedest, most extravagant daughters in the world. They're the children of his first marriage. They are proud and haughty and they waste the money of the realm as though it were so much sand. The people are crying out against them and their wasteful ways but the prince seems unable to curb them. The prince has a third daughter, the child of his second wife. Her name is Angelina and she certainly is as good and beautiful as an angel. We call her the Princess Linka. There isn't a man in the country that wouldn't go through fire and water for her--God bless her! As for the other two--may the Devil take them!"

Suddenly remembering himself, the landlord clapped his hand to his mouth in alarm.

Peter laughed good-humoredly.

"That's all right, landlord. Don't mind me. As I've told you before I'm not the Devil. I'm only his little brother-in-law."

The landlord shook his head.

"Yes, I know, but I must say it seems much the same to me."

One afternoon the prince came riding down to the tavern and asked for Peter. He was horrified at first by Peter's appearance, but he treated him most politely, invited him to the castle, and ended by begging the loan of a large sum of money.

Peter said to the prince:

"I'll give you as much money as you want provided you let me marry one of your daughters."

The prince wasn't prepared for this but he needed money so badly that he said:

"H'm, which one of them?"

"I'm not particular," Peter answered. "Any of them will do."

When he gave the prince some money in advance, the prince agreed and Peter promised to come to the castle the next day to meet his bride to be.

The prince when he got home told his daughters that he had seen Peter. They questioned him about Peter's appearance and asked him what sort of a looking person this brother-in-law of the Devil was.

"He isn't so very ugly," the prince said, "really he isn't. If he washed his face and trimmed his hair and nails he'd be fairly good-looking. In fact I rather like him."

He then talked to them very seriously about the state of the treasury and he told them that unless he could raise a large sum of money shortly there was danger of an uprising among the people.

"If you, my daughters, wish to see the peace of the country preserved, if you want to make me happy in my old age, one of you will have to marry this young man, for I see no other way to raise the money."

At this the two older princesses tossed their heads scornfully and laughed loud and long.

"You may rest assured, dear father, that neither of

us will marry such a creature! We are the daughters of a prince and won't marry beneath us, no, not even to save the country from ruin!"

"Then I don't know what I'll do," the prince said.

"Father," whispered Linka, the youngest. Her voice quavered and her face turned pale. "Father, if your happiness and the peace of the country depend on this marriage, I will sacrifice myself, God help me!"

"My child! My dear child!" the prince cried, taking Linka in his arms and kissing her tenderly.

The two elder sisters jeered and ha-ha-ed.

"Little sister-in-law of the Devil!" they said mockingly. "Now if you were to marry Prince Lucifer himself that would be something, for at least you would be a princess! But only to be his sister-in-law--ha! ha!--what does that amount to?"

And they laughed with amusement and made nasty evil jokes until poor little Linka had to put her hands to her ears not to hear them.

The next day Peter came to the castle. The older sisters when they saw how black he was were glad enough they had refused to marry him. As for Linka, the moment she looked at him she fainted dead away.

When she revived the prince led her over to Peter and gave Peter her hand. She was trembling violently and her hand was cold as marble.

"Don't be afraid, little princess," Peter whispered to her gently. "I know how awful I look. But perhaps I won't always be so ugly. I promise you, if you marry me, I shall always love you dearly."

Linka was greatly comforted by the sound of his pleasant voice, but each time she looked at him she was terrified anew.

Peter saw this and made his visit short. He handed out to the prince as much money as he needed and then, after agreeing to return in eight days for the wedding, he hurried off.

He went to the place where he had met the Devil the first time and called him by name with all his might.

The Devil instantly appeared.

"What do you want, little brother-in-law?"

"I want to look like myself again," Peter said. "What good will it do me to marry a sweet little princess and then have the poor girl faint away every time she looks at me!"

"Very well, brother-in-law. If that is how you feel about it, come along with me and I'll soon make you into a handsome young man."

Peter leaped on the Devil's back and off they flew over mountains and forests and distant countries.

They alighted in a deep forest beside a bubbling spring.

"Now, little brother-in-law," the Devil said, "wash in this water and see how handsome you'll soon be."

Peter threw off his clothes and jumped into the water and when he came out his skin was as beautiful and fresh as a girl's. He looked at his own reflection in the spring and it made him so happy that he said to the Devil:

"Brother-in-law, I'm more grateful to you for this than for all the money you've given me. Now my dear Linka will love me!"

He put his arms about the Devil's neck and off they flew once again. This time they went to a big city where Peter bought beautiful clothes and jewels and coaches and horses. He engaged servants in fine livery and, when he was ready to go to his bride, he had a following that was worthy of any prince.

At the castle the Princess Linka paced her chamber pale and trembling. The two older sisters were with her, laughing heartlessly and making evil jokes, and running every moment to the window to see if the groom were coming.

At last they saw in the distance a long line of shining coaches with outriders in rich livery. The coaches drew up at the castle gate and from the first one a handsome youth, arrayed like a prince, alighted. He hurried into the castle and ran straight upstairs to Linka's chamber.

At first Linka was afraid to look at him for she
supposed he was still black. But when he took her
hand and whispered: "Dear Linka, look at me now
and you won't be frightened," she looked and it
seemed to her that Peter was the very handsomest
young man in all the world. She fell in love with
him on sight and I might as well tell you she's been
in love with him ever since.

The two older sisters stood at the window frozen
stiff with envy and surprise. Suddenly they felt
some one clutch them from behind. They turned in
fright and who did they see standing there but the
Devil himself!

"Don't be afraid, my dear brides," he said. "I'm not a
common fellow. I'm Prince Lucifer himself. So, in
becoming my brides you are not losing rank!"

Then he turned to Peter and chuckled.

"You see now, Peter, why you are my brother-in-
law. You're marrying one sister and I'm taking the
other two!"

With that he picked up the two wicked sisters under
his arm and puff! with a whiff of sulphur they all
three disappeared through the ceiling.

The Princess Linka as she clung to her young
husband asked a little fearfully:

"Peter, do you suppose we'll have to see our
brother-in-law often?"

"Not if you make me a good wife," Peter said.

And you can understand what a good wife Linka became when I tell you that never again all her life long did she see the Devil.

THE SHOEMAKER'S APRON

THE STORY OF THE MAN WHO SITS NEAR THE GOLDEN GATE

There was once a shoemaker who made so little at his trade that his wife suffered and his children went hungry. In desperation he offered to sell his soul to a devil.

"How much do you want for your soul?" the devil asked him.

"I want work enough to give me a good livelihood," the shoemaker said, "so that my wife won't suffer nor my children starve."

The devil agreed to this and the shoemaker put his mark on the contract. After that trade improved and soon the little shoemaker was happy and prosperous.

Now one night it happened that Christ and the blessed St. Peter, who were walking about on earth, stopped at the little shoemaker's cottage and asked for a night's lodging. The shoemaker received them most hospitably. He had his wife cook them a fine supper and after supper he gave them his own bed to sleep on while he and his wife went to the garret and slept on straw.

In the morning he had his wife prepare them a good breakfast and after breakfast he took them on their way for a mile or two.

As he was leaving them, St. Peter whispered to Christ:

"Master, this poor man has given us of his best. Don't you think you ought to reward him?"

Christ nodded and, turning to the little shoemaker, he said:

"For your kindness to us this day I will reward you. Make three wishes and they will be granted."

The shoemaker thanked Christ and said:

"Well then, these are my wishes: first, may whoever sits down on my cobbler's stool be unable to get up until I permit him; second, may whoever looks into the window of my cottage have to stand there until I let him go; and third, may whoever shakes the pear-tree in my garden stick to the tree until I set him free."

"Your wishes will be granted," Christ promised. Then he and St. Peter went on their way and the shoemaker returned to his cottage.

The years went by and at last one afternoon the devil stood before the shoemaker and said:

"Ho, shoemaker, your time has come! Are you ready?"

"Just let me have a bite of supper first," the shoemaker said. "In the meantime you sit down here on my stool and rest yourself."

The devil who had been walking up and down the earth since sunrise was tired and so was glad enough to sit down.

After supper the little shoemaker said:

"Now then, I'm ready. Come on."

The devil tried to stand up but of course he couldn't. He pulled this way and that. He stretched, he rolled from side to side until his bones ached, but all to no avail. He could not get up from the stool.

"Brother!" he cried in terror, "help me off this cursed stool and I'll give you seven more years--I swear I will!"

At that promise the shoemaker allowed the devil to stand up, and the devil scurried off as fast as he could.

He was true to his word. He didn't come back for seven years. When he did come he was too clever to risk sitting down again on the cobbler's stool. He didn't even venture inside the cottage door. Instead, he stood at the window and called out:

"Ho, shoemaker, here I am again! Your time has come! Are you ready?"

"I'll be ready in a moment," the shoemaker said, "Just let me put a last stitch in these shoes."

When the shoemaker had finished sewing the shoes, he put aside his work, bade his wife good-bye, and said to the devil:

"Now then, I'm ready. Let us go."

But the devil when he tried to move away from the window found that he was held fast. It was as if his feet had been soldered to the earth. In great fright he cried out:

"Oh, my dear little shoemaker, help me! I can't move!"

"What's this trick you're playing on me?" the shoemaker said. "Now I'm ready to go and you aren't! What do you mean by making a fool of me this way?"

"Just help me to get free," the devil cried, "and I'll do anything in the world for you! I'll give you seven more years! I swear I will!"

"Very well," the shoemaker said, "then I'll help you this time. But never again! Now remember: I won't let you make a fool of me a third time!"

So the shoemaker freed the devil from the window and the devil without another word scurried off.

At the end of another seven years he appeared again. But this time he was too clever to look in the window. He didn't even come near the cottage. Instead he stood off in the garden under the pear-tree and called out:

"Ho, there, shoemaker! Your time has come and I am here to get you! Are you ready?"

"I'll be ready in a moment," the shoemaker said. "Just wait until I put away my tools. If you feel like it, shake yourself down a nice ripe pear."

The devil shook the pear-tree and of course when he tried to stop he couldn't. He shook until all the pears had fallen. He kept on and presently he had shaken off all the leaves.

When the shoemaker came out and saw the tree stripped and bare and the devil still shaking it, he pretended to fall into a fearful rage.

"Hi, there, you! What do you mean shaking down all my pears! Stop it! Do you hear me? Stop it!"

"But I can't stop it!" the poor devil cried.

"We'll see about that!" the shoemaker said.

He ran back into the cottage and got a long leather strap. Then he began beating the devil unmercifully over his head and shoulders.

The devil made such an outcry that all the village heard him and came running to see what was the matter.

"Help! Help!" the devil cried. "Make the shoemaker

stop beating me!"

But all the people thought the shoemaker was doing just right to punish the black fellow for shaking down all his pears and they urged the shoemaker to beat him harder.

"My poor head! My poor shoulders!" the devil moaned. "If ever I get loose from this cursed pear-tree I'll never come back here! I swear I won't!"

The shoemaker, when he heard this, laughed in his sleeve and let the devil go.

The devil was true to his word. He never again returned. So the shoemaker lived, untroubled, to a ripe old age.

Just before he died he asked that his cobbler's apron be buried with him and his sons carried out his wish.

As soon as he died the little shoemaker trudged up to heaven and knocked timidly at the golden gate. St. Peter opened the gate a little crack and peeped out. When he saw the shoemaker he shook his head and said:

"Little shoemaker, heaven is no place for you. While you were alive you sold your soul to the ruler of the other place and now you must go there."

With that St. Peter shut the golden gate and locked it.

The little shoemaker sighed and said to himself:

"Well, I suppose I must go where St. Peter says."

So he put on a bold front and tramped down to hell.
When the devil who knew him saw him coming, he
shouted out to his fellow devils:

"Brothers, on guard! Here comes that terrible little
shoemaker! Lock every gate! Don't let him in or
he'll drive us all out of hell!"

The devils in great fright scurried about and locked
and barred all the gates, and the little shoemaker
when he arrived could not get in.

He knocked and knocked but no one would answer.

"They don't seem to want me here," he said to
himself. "I suppose I'll have to try heaven again."

So he trudged back to St. Peter and explained to
him that hell was locked up tight.

"No matter," St. Peter said. "As I told you before
heaven is no place for you."

The little shoemaker, tired and dejected, went back
to hell but again the devils, when they saw him
coming, locked every gate and kept him out.

In desperation the little shoemaker returned to
heaven and pounded loudly on the golden gate.
Thinking from the noise that some very important

saint had arrived, St. Peter flung open the gate. Quick as a flash the little shoemaker threw his leather apron inside, then hopped in himself under St. Peter's elbow and squatted down on the apron.

In great excitement St. Peter tried to turn him out of heaven, but the little shoemaker shouted:

"You can't touch me! You can't touch me! I'm sitting on my own property! Let me alone!"

He raised such a hubbub that all the angels and the blessed saints came running to see what was happening. Presently Lord Jesus himself came and the little shoemaker explained to him how he just had to stay in heaven as the devils wouldn't let him into hell.

"Now, Master," St. Peter said, "what am I to do? You know yourself we can't keep this fellow in heaven."

But Lord Jesus, looking with pity on the poor little shoemaker, said to St. Peter:

"Just let him stay where he is. He won't bother any one sitting here near the gate."

Made in the USA
Monee, IL
15 December 2020

52944125R00115